RUFUS WHO?

Rufus Who?

KESTER BRANFORD

UPFRONT PUBLISHING
LEICESTERSHIRE

Rufus Who?
Copyright © Kester Branford 2003

ISBN 1-84426-109-3

First published 2003 by
UPFRONT PUBLISHING LTD
Leicestershire

Typeset in Bembo by
Bookcraft Ltd, Stroud, Gloucestershire
Printed by Lightning Source

Contents

Rainflies and Twinkle 1

The Red House 10

Tobago 45

Belmont Circular Road 55

Sally 70

Carmen 82

The Red House, Again 124

The Royal Gaol 140

Uncle Cyril 186

Rainflies and Twinkle

Whenever he heard that sound, he knew what was going to happen next. Whenever he heard that unique rumble, so faint in the distance, he was willing to bet any amount of money that some of the neighbours would be rushing outside to grab the clothes off the line, and that, within a matter of seconds, some of the boys would be rushing outside to shower in the rain. At the side of the house where there was no gutter, the water would be cascading down from the corrugations in the roof and collecting in puddles of mud. The other side of the house would be less spectacular. There the gutter receiving the water would be evacuating it into a downspout, which in turn would be disgorging it into a huge steel barrel. But soon the overflow from the barrel would be forming more puddles of mud. By then, what had been a faint rumble as the rain swooped in from the east would have reached a crescendo, and he could curl up in bed and savour the racket which he so enjoyed – the utterly unmistakable crash of the rain pounding on the rooftops as if the raindrops were trying to drill holes through the corrugated iron. He was never bothered by any doubts on the matter; whenever he heard that unique rumble, he knew exactly what was going to happen next.

Among the talents Uncle Clive proudly showed off when watching cricket from the uncovered stands at the Queen's Park Oval was the unerring ability to predict how long it was going to rain. Rufus was a close understudy. If he happened to be out in the street playing cricket, he might look reflectively at the sky, examine the clouds, judge which way the wind was blowing, then proclaim in an oracular tone that there would only be a passing downpour. He might even offer odds of five to one that the sun would be back to its normal blistering and scorching ways in less than half an hour. For Rufus loved to bet.

Today he didn't dare challenge Auntie Mavis to a wager. She had been in a foul mood since returning from the 5 a.m. mass. She was always in fine mettle and full of vitality when she woke up early on Sunday morning to get ready for church. She used to tell Rufus (and he was only too happy to take her word for it) that the smell of the dew was sweetest in the pre-dawn hours of a Sunday. She needed no alarm clock. Hers was built in, and however exhausted she might be, she could set it to wake her at any hour she chose – even long before the roosters started waking up everybody else. Her internal alarm clock was remarkably reliable, and had never failed her, as far as Rufus knew.

While she couldn't explain why she preferred the 5 o'clock mass to all others, she observed that she was not alone in that predilection. Sunday after Sunday, she encountered or noticed other 5 o'clock regulars who could be kept away only by serious illness or (God forbid!) death. But then there were the other patrons, some just bleary-eyed, some also reeking of alcohol, who religiously stopped by on their way home from some sinfully delightful party. Auntie Mavis hardly paid any attention to them.

As she was subsequently to relate to Rufus, she became vaguely aware of a commotion somewhere towards the back of the church sometime after the priest had said the Creed. From the acrid smell offending the noses of the congregationers during the Consecration, she had surmised that someone had been sick. It was only after the mass, as she was about to greet one of the 5 o'clock regulars, that she had seen the someone. Hours

2

later, she was still devastated with rage at the sight of her nephew Tony, the same Tony who used to live in her house, stretched out on the floor and being fanned energetically by a young lady she did not recognize. She did not know that Tony had started going back to church. While he was under her roof, she had suspected that he helped himself to her whisky, but she would never have guessed that he would consume so much liquor that he would vomit and pass out in church.

More often than not, Auntie Mavis would emerge from the 5 o'clock mass feeling exhilarated, all ready to get the black pudding going in the frying-pan. Today Rufus found the black pudding all burnt and Auntie Mavis all fuming. So he dared not challenge her to a wager.

He would undoubtedly have lost if he had bet on a downpour of short duration. His delight in the pounding sound of the rain began to abate after he had been curled up in bed with his book for over an hour and a half, and the rainflies started to come out. They materialized when it rained long and hard – sometimes, not every time. By some mysterious act of creation, they appeared by the dozen, leaving a mess behind as they lost their wings and crawled about aimlessly, looking like so many over-sized ants. Rufus couldn't imagine what point there could be to their ephemeral, rain-induced existence, unless it was to vary the diet of the lizards and spare them the trouble of stalking the ordinary houseflies. As he flicked a rainfly off his ankle, he found himself musing about them and about how they didn't seem to have much of a life. It occurred to him, too, that he had never been able to fathom where they came from. But he, after all, was no better off; he was just like them in that respect – or just like his dog Twinkle, for that matter.

When Rufus was nine, Twinkle had latched itself on to him in a way that suggested they were meant to be together. Early one

Saturday morning, on his way back from a shop where he had gone to buy bread, he noticed that he was being followed by a tiny, ugly puppy which could not have been more than a few weeks old. Rufus stamped his foot menacingly, and picked up a stone as if to throw it at the puppy, but the latter just wagged its tail and appeared to wink at Rufus. In fact, the puppy was not winking; it had only one eye. At any rate, it must have been a case of love at second sight, for Rufus's heart melted, and he permitted the puppy to follow him all the way into Auntie Mavis's kitchen, where it immediately claimed and marked the scuffed linoleum as its territory. Auntie Mavis walked in to find Rufus feverishly cleaning up the mess.

'I want no pothounds in or around this house,' she declared at once.

'Pothounds' was the word that everybody used in reference to the stray mongrels that were reviled for their reputed ability to sniff food out – from miles away. They compensated for their undistinguished ancestry with a sense of smell no less keen than that of the bloodhound or foxhound, but the only scent they picked up and tracked with any assiduity or alacrity was that of a pot on the fire. Their nose was well matched by ears sharply attuned, also from miles away, to the scraping of plates heralding the dumping of leftovers. And their nightly overturning of dust-bins as they foraged for food had earned them a reputation as scavengers. In short, every nine-year-old knew that a dog called a pothound was not being complimented, and the tears welling up in Rufus's eyes told Auntie Mavis that he was bitterly stung by the offensive appellation.

'I want no stray dog in or around this house,' she said. Then, noticing that it was a female, she added:

'All the dogs in the area are going to be coming into our yard.'

Auntie Mavis was forced to admit to herself that she found the animal's appearance off-putting. Indeed the puppy couldn't accurately be described as being cuddly. On the contrary, she was strikingly unprepossessing. Her snout protruded far beyond what seemed normal, and her right eye was permanently closed. Compounding the asymmetrical effect, one ear drooped, while the other pointed upwards. And her white fur was blemished by bald patches distributed at random along her back. So diseased did she appear that Auntie Mavis could barely bring herself to look at her.

'Take it outside, and keep the door closed,' she ordered.

Unremittingly, the puppy whined and clawed at the door as her fate was being discussed in the kitchen. The question of food was the first that arose. Auntie Mavis had the strange notion that table scraps would suffice. Rufus had the equally strange notion that some special dog-food, which no doubt could be bought at certain stores in Port-of-Spain, would be essential to ensuring proper growth.

'I have no money to spend on a dog. I am not going to waste my good, hard-earned money on any dog-food. If she stays, she will just have to eat leftovers, like all the other dogs in this country.'

'A little puppy like this can't eat leftovers,' Rufus pleaded. 'She will choke to death!'

'Give her some milk. Put some bread in it. Stale bread. Or you can take her back right where you found her.'

Rarely did Auntie Mavis display so much irritation in speaking to Rufus, and he knew from the sharpness of her tone that he shouldn't press his luck. He got permission to take an old bowl from under the kitchen sink, and prepared a meal for the puppy. When he observed how she devoured the preparation of stale bread bloated with milk, he concluded that she didn't mind not having proper dog-food bought at a store. Maybe he himself would eventually come to terms with the unhappy situation.

Then there was the question of the work involved in caring for a sickly puppy. Auntie Mavis was afraid that she would be saddled with the unwelcome responsibility.

Rufus was persistent and beseeching: 'I will take care of her. I will do all the work. I promise!'

Auntie Mavis gave in, but as she did so, she was already preparing herself for the day when Rufus would break his promise. But he was to surprise her.

He wasted no time in taking charge, going about his task with a sense of purpose that Auntie Mavis had not yet seen in her nine-year-old nephew. He spent the remainder of the morning looking for the ideal bed. When he finally located the perfect old cardboard box, he spent the afternoon in the backyard, performing a paint job that was a veritable labour of love – red paint on the inside of the box, white on the outside. After arranging some newspaper bedding in the box, he went into his room with even more newspaper, which he proceeded to spread on the floor. Then he went back out to fetch the box, no longer dripping with paint, but still wet, and headed towards his room again.

'Where do you think you are going with that?' Auntie Mavis asked.

Rufus knew that the only satisfactory answer to the question was a quick about-turn, so he made one, then lingered near the kitchen, still carrying the cardboard box.

Auntie Mavis was unyielding: 'That dog is going to have to stay outside. I don't want her anywhere in this house.'

There wasn't much point in arguing. He would choose a spot under the house, directly below his room, as the site for the puppy's bed.

Rufus hurried down the steps at the side of the house, and the puppy, still in attendance outside the kitchen door, scurried after him. There was reason to hurry, for it was already late evening, and the fleeting twilight would be yielding, as abruptly as usual, to the darkness that would soon envelop the land. He hoped that he would finish putting the puppy to bed before it got pitch-dark. Ever since his cousin Pearl had told him that spirits lived under the house, he avoided being there after sunset, which was when the spirits came out in force.

It was difficult to get the puppy to stay in the cardboard box. As long as Rufus stroked her head, she was content to lie still, but as soon as he stopped and moved away, she jumped out and stuck to his heels, with a piteous whimper. He resigned himself to the prospect of being caught by darkness under the house. According to Pearl, cats, dogs and lots of other animals could see the spirits, and could actually keep them at bay. Pearl claimed that by smearing one's finger with mucus from a dog's eyes and rubbing it into one's own eyes, one could acquire what she called 'spirit vision' and see all manner of supernatural creatures. Rufus therefore took great care not to let his fingers get too close to the puppy's eye.

As he looked at the mournful face of his all-seeing protector, her eye boring into him and twinkling in the descending darkness like a tiny, solitary bulb on a Christmas tree, the name 'Twinkle' came to him as one that fitted her naturally and perfectly. So he said over and over in a soothing tone as he stroked her head:

'Stay, Twinkle. Go to sleep.'

It must have been the magical power of the name that worked the charm; Twinkle stayed in the box. But that night, and for many nights to come, she cried herself to sleep.

As far as taking care of Twinkle was concerned, Rufus was true to his word. No doubt the preparation of bread and milk, supplemented by choice leftovers, was better than what any veterinary surgeon could have ordered. With lavish attention as a tonic, Twinkle's recovery and growth were phenomenal, and in a couple of months, Rufus had forgotten how scrawny and sickly she used to look. Since everything led him to believe that she had the makings of a guard dog, he was anxious to display a 'Beware of the dog' sign. In the meantime, he was pleased with the way she responded to his 'Sick!' by snarling at passing cars and unwelcome dogs.

Having managed to persuade Auntie Mavis to buy a special hairbrush, he started devoting an inordinate amount of his spare time to the grooming of Twinkle, who continued to thrive. The next item he wanted Auntie Mavis to buy for Twinkle was a toothbrush, but there she drew the line.

'How is that dog going to brush her teeth?' she asked drily. 'Why don't you go and brush your own.'

She was wrong to assume that Rufus was just pushing his luck. Hers was clearly a false view of the situation. Twinkle did indeed have bad breath, and Rufus began to be bothered by it the very first time he tried training her to fetch objects. With enthusiasm, she bounded off in the direction of the stick that he flung a few yards away, but before she could bring it all the way back to him, it dropped out of her mouth. Not the least bit deterred, she kept running towards him with her tongue hanging out and her tail swirling. As she panted, she exhaled her breath in his face, and despite his love for her, he found it intolerably foul.

Since this was something to be attended to urgently, why couldn't he use an old toothbrush? There was never any scarcity of such toothbrushes about the house. It seemed that few toothbrushes were ever thrown out by Auntie Mavis. When their bristles were too worn and misshapen to be effective in cleaning teeth, they were assigned to the new task of applying polish to shoes. Rufus knew exactly where to find some that were lying idle, awaiting their new assignment. Contemplating that embarrassment of toothbrushes, he thought and did the unthinkable: he selected for the mouth of his beloved Twinkle a toothbrush that had seen better days in Auntie Mavis's mouth and was destined for a shoe!

Twinkle would have none of it, and Rufus failed to brush her teeth, try as he might. Although he prized open her mouth for a fleeting instant, she wriggled free and bolted in order to avoid further torture. A different approach would have to be tried if the problem of the stink mouth was to be solved.

It never was. That was one of a number of unfulfilled plans concerning Twinkle. How he would have loved to build a dog house for her, to give her serious obedience training so that she would obey his commands, to break her out of the habit of jumping on people, chewing up Auntie Mavis's shoes, marauding through the neighbourhood and investigating dustbins!

He tried to take his mind off the subject of Twinkle. Often it did his heart a lot of good to relive the many truly delightful memories of Twinkle. What was painful was to remember how she was killed. He was convinced that it was because of her fondness for dustbins that she was killed, and though he would never be able to prove it, he was equally convinced that Mr Scobie had poisoned her. His intuition told him so ... But he really didn't want to think about it. More pressing claims on his attention were being made by the business at hand: how to tell Auntie Mavis about what had happened at the Red House.

The Red House

Of course, Rufus had often wondered about his parents. To be exact, he had wondered how his life would have been with his mother, and why his father treated him as he did. He would fantasize about life with his mother, the fantasy beginning the day he was born, the generous details about labour being furnished by memories of what he had read or heard somewhere. In one scenario, she would be in labour for exactly 24 hours. The exactness of the figure pleased him. Towards the end of the twenty-third hour, the doctor would suddenly become aware of a hitherto unsuspected complication. An early variant of this scenario, in which Rufus's father would be the one to alert the doctor, was discarded when Rufus heard that in those days fathers were kept out of the delivery room. But in both cases, the doctor would work the miracle, later recounting to his colleagues that had he intervened one second later, the woman would have died in childbirth.

In another scenario, Rufus's mother would go into premature labour while travelling in a taxi from downtown Port-of-Spain to Belmont. The taxi-driver would discharge and refund all the other passengers and rush her to the General Hospital. There the doctor would later recount to his colleagues that had the taxi arrived one second later, the woman would have died in childbirth.

There were times, though, when Rufus did wish that his mother had died in childbirth. He would have preferred the certainty of her death to the continuing mystery of her where-abouts. At the age of six, when, thinking it strange that he, of all the children around him, could identify no one of the women who frequented his Auntie Mavis's house as his mother, he had put the question to Auntie Mavis. The original simple answer that his mother was temporarily in Venezuela had over the years become more disconcerting in response to his more probing inquiries. By the age of 11, Rufus felt he had the full distressing story, and asked no further questions of those around him. His mother had abandoned him as a baby and now lived somewhere in Venezuela. At school, during the week preceding Mother's Day, red poppies would be worn by boys whose mothers were alive, white poppies by those whose mothers were dead. Rufus never bought any.

He got used to hearing his grandmother marvel at the close physical resemblance between such-and-such a grandchild and such-and-such a remote ancestor, or at some mannerism that was a throwback to another remote ancestor. She couldn't suppress her exultation when she succeeded in identifying first-known sources and tracing lines of descent. 'Blood can't hide,' she would declare triumphantly. In the case of Rufus, the blood did seem to hide. She never said who he took after or who he inherited his perfect pitch from.

Before applying for his birth certificate, it had never occurred to Rufus to inquire about his mother's name. But then again, he had gone to the Red House totally unprepared for his first trying encounter with bureaucracy. He made it to the first queue without the slightest difficulty, and spent his fifty minutes listening with increasing anxiety to the disrespectful comments of the less-patient applicants about the work attitudes of civil servants. His attention was drawn to a woman of skeletal build who kept pacing up and down. About every five minutes or so, she would stop pacing and stand erect and motionless for a few moments, drawing the very deepest of breaths. She was angular all over, except for her nose, which was amazingly snub. Her jump-suit complemented her bony frame and made her look like a pilot. The outfit was unbecoming and fetching at the same time. It was her tone, distinctly raucous and irate, that had attracted Rufus's attention. Her pacing was in unison with her ranting, the latter helping her to display teeth that gleamed in two even rows, with several glints of gold.

'Christmas hardly over and they thinking 'bout Carnival,' she complained. 'The Government should fire all o' them!'

It was apparent to Rufus, too, that the various clerks who were nonchalantly milling about and chatting behind the counter were concentrating on things that had nothing to do with serving the public. Yet he was more inclined – far more inclined than the roving protester – to commiserate with them; it was, after all, the height of the festive season – the twenty-seventh of December, and a Friday at that. As a teacher, Rufus was spared the dreadful experience of going back out immediately after Boxing Day and working to the pervasive sounds of Christmas parang music. Moved by such empathy, he decided to be polite and cheerful, and tried out his merriest 'Good morning' on a clerk with a short Afro with whom he came face to face at the counter. She failed to acknowledge his greeting and went straight to the point:

'You have your stamps?'

'What stamps?'

'Your four 50-cent stamps. I can't give you the form if you don't have four 50-cent stamps.'

Rufus felt ashamed of his ignorance, but brave enough to protest:

'How was I supposed to know about these stamps? You all should put up a sign or something so people will know not to waste their time lining up before they get the stamps. You mean to say you can't give me the form now and let me come back straight to you with the stamps?'

'Mister, a lot of people waiting behind you, and besides, you holding up the line.'

Rufus could tell when he was being dismissed. Joined by two other ignorant applicants, he went in search of four 50-cent stamps.

By the time they returned, a jovial-looking young man had replaced the woman with the short Afro. Rufus fantasized that she had been summarily dismissed for giving him the run-around, and strode confidently to the jovial-looking young man, ignoring the accusations of queue-jumping from the patient applicants.

'Like you didn't see all the people waiting in front of you?' said the jovial-looking young man.

'I was in the line before, and the woman who was here said I had to get some stamps.'

'You know how many people try that trick when they don't want to line up?' inquired the jovial-looking young man, with a reproachful smile.

Rufus was beginning to lose patience.

'Look, the time we stand up here talking, you could have given me the form already.'

'And then people will say how I deal with my friends first, when people waiting long time before them.'

Sounds of approval of such sternness began to be heard from the line of patient applicants.

Rufus bit his lip, ground his teeth and never unclenched his jaw as he waited another forty-five minutes behind them. He cast his most murderous glare at the jovial-looking young man, who handed him the form with an encouraging 'Good things come to those who wait.'

With his quick perusal of the application form, Rufus's ignorance of his mother's name descended upon him and placed him in a dilemma. Since he lacked that crucial detail, the form couldn't be completed unless he was briefed by Auntie Mavis. But he hadn't told her of his plans, and he didn't want to go to her office just to find out his mother's name. He looked in the direction of the clerk who was receiving the completed forms, looked at the length of the queue, and decided to chance it. Maybe he wouldn't need to fill in every line of the application form – if the clerk was amenable enough. He was in luck. Before he had spent twenty minutes in the new queue, he heard someone call out to him from behind the counter, and recognized Gregory, otherwise known as 'Pinhead'.

'What happening, Gregory man?' Rufus inquired, thinking it better not to use the more familiar appellation in this official place of government business. But Pinhead frowned and looked irritated.

'I don't want nobody to call me by my slave name again, Rufus. My liberation name is Ngobi. Zala Ngobi.'

'Sorry, man. I didn't realize. But how come you working in here, man? I thought you were in England or one of them dread places.'

Pinhead and Rufus had entered the first form the same year and had remained good friends throughout their stay at the College. Two years older than Rufus, precocious and wise in the ways of the world, Pinhead had always been something of a rebel and an activist. From his earliest days at the College, he was trying to dissuade his mates from wearing the blazers required on special occasions:

'Not suitable for the tropics,' he insisted.

He did manage, on one occasion, to organize a blazer-less group of eight. All eight were sent home for the day, and

Pinhead, as ring-leader, was given five days of detention to boot.

At the start of 1970, Pinhead was ebullient, truly in his element as he put on the mantle of militant. Rufus could still picture him all flushed with excitement when, towards the end of February, demonstrators took over the Roman Catholic Cathedral. Pinhead was the one who broke the news to the fifth form, just after recess one afternoon, that Archbishop Pantin was being invited to join a Black Power march. Day in, day out, he proclaimed that Eric Williams was about to be overthrown.

'Mark my words,' he intoned, 'The writing is on the wall. Black Power will be the downfall of Eric!'

Then he took it into his head to start organizing what later became known as the 'rallies at recess' outside the canteen. He urged everyone to resist the temptation to rush off in search of Popsicles or aloo pies during the short break. Instead, they should all come and listen to him in order to find out what was going to happen to the country. He confidently declared that his prophecies would be fulfilled: that a state of emergency and a curfew would be imposed, that 'Eric will turn the country into a police State to save his own skin'. One day he called on the whole student body to march out of school and around the Queen's Park Savannah. No one responded to the call, so eventually Pinhead marched out by himself. The principal suspended him for a week, and called in his parents.

The Pinhead who returned from suspension was subdued and reticent. He began to absent himself with increasing frequency, though he never failed to hand in a written excuse in a sealed envelope. He spoke to no one, not even his closest friends, about the reasons for his absences. Rufus speculated that either Pinhead or someone in his household must be gravely ill. The facts were to be revealed later, and then Rufus, with the benefit of hindsight, was to claim that he had known all along what was going on. He was only lying.

It was nearing the end of the last period on a Tuesday afternoon when the principal received a telephone call from someone at Police Headquarters trying to ascertain whether Pinhead was a student at the school. He was asked to come to Headquarters to identify Pinhead.

According to Pinhead's version of the incident, he had been demonstrating on Frederick Street with some Black Power marchers when he made a comment about the knock knees of a constable on patrol. The constable challenged him to repeat the comment, and Pinhead looked him straight in the eye and said:

'If you only lay a finger on me, it's assault and battery.'

The constable flew into a rage, Pinhead flew into a rage, and in the ensuing altercation about who would assault and batter whom, shoves and blows were exchanged. Pinhead was taken away to Headquarters to be charged with assaulting an officer of the law. But then another officer recognized Pinhead's surname to be that of an affluent, influential and well-known family. After consultations with a senior officer and further questioning of Pinhead, the principal of the College was contacted.

No charges were laid, and the principal drove Pinhead home. He contemplated the impressive assortment of fruit trees around him as he waited on the veranda for Pinhead's parents. His mind was made up: the boy had to be removed from the College.

If Pinhead's parents were surprised or upset to learn that instead of going to school, he had been marching and demonstrating up and down the country, they didn't show it. Not even his admission that he had written the excuses himself and forged his father's signature ruffled them. It wasn't the principal who brought up the question of Pinhead's future at the College; they themselves offered to place him elsewhere.

16

When he was not at school, Rufus had next to no contact with his schoolmates. As Auntie Mavis's telephone was often out of order, it was seldom used. There was the pro forma exchange of cards at Christmas, but no exchange of visits at any time. Although the friendship between Pinhead and Rufus was of long standing, neither had ever been to the other's home. Rufus was therefore greatly surprised to receive a letter from Pinhead, and then to read that he was being invited to Pinhead's home. He did not expect it at all. In the letter, Pinhead rambled about the meaning of the struggle for emancipation, and the value of commitment and sacrifice. The final paragraph contained a simple request: he wanted Rufus to bring the books and other items from his desk.

'Pick the padlock,' he wrote. 'If you can't pick it, break it.'

In the event, Rufus did have to break the lock, but only after he had managed to destroy measuring-compasses, paper clips and hairpins in attempting to pick it. And all that he found in the desk was a geometry set and three publications: a sex manual, a history of Africa and a magazine with a picture of Fidel Castro on the cover.

Predictably enough, when Rufus took up the receiver to call Pinhead, the phone was out of order, so he asked Auntie Mavis to call from her office. She got directions to Pinhead's house and offered to drive Rufus there. On the way, he reflected that he was fortunate not to have to find his own way. The boys at school would have said that Pinhead lived behind God's back. Indeed the house was far off the beaten track, far from the roads along which the buses and route taxis plied. Auntie Mavis drove all the way through Maraval, then turned on to a dirt road that bisected a cocoa plantation. It was a smooth ride – no ruts, no pot-holes, just well-compacted dirt. After what must have been at least two miles of cocoa pods and occasional bunches of bananas dragging down their host trees, they came to a steep hill with palatial houses tucked away amid an array of fruit trees and towering immortelle trees in full bloom. The air was ripe with the smell of guava and soursop, but it was not still. The engine strained as the car laboured up the hill, and the approach of the strangers was being heralded by dogs relaying the message from yard to yard with their barking. As the car passed by, colossal Alsatians and Dobermann pinschers flung themselves on to the gates and fences enclosing their territory, some snarling, some barking, all looking belligerent, ferocious and eager to tear Rufus apart.

Pinhead, having no doubt heard the canine announcement, was standing expectantly at the open gates of his private orchard. Auntie Mavis was able to drive straight in without further agitating the dogs across the street.

'Hold your dogs!' said Rufus, not yet daring to step out of the car.

Pinhead had heard that line before. He laughed and said what he always said in response:

'Not to worry. We don't have any dogs and we don't need to. We let all the neighbours' dogs guard our house for us.'

Something in Pinhead's manner suggested to Auntie Mavis that they should not stay long, so when he invited her in, she said she would wait in the car. He didn't press her further. He chatted for a while with Rufus on the veranda, talked about the marches, the demonstrations, and the incident with the policeman. He also disclosed that his parents were sending him to England to do his O Levels. Soon, however, Rufus too began to sense that he was overstaying his welcome, and excused himself by saying he didn't want to keep his aunt waiting. Pinhead understood. Rufus formed the conclusion that Pinhead was uneasy and embarrassed to be seen living in luxury, and that's the interpretation he offered to Auntie Mavis on the way back.

During the five years that had since elapsed, Rufus had heard that Pinhead was repeatedly failing his GCE examinations in England. He had also heard a rumour that Pinhead had once gone to Cuba to help with a sugar harvest. But he didn't know that Pinhead was back in Trinidad. Curious to know how he had landed a civil-service job when he couldn't even get his O Levels, Rufus ventured to ask how things had been in England.

'It's the cold I can't take, man. I want to be out here sweating in the hot sun and closer to my roots. A man mustn't stay away from his roots.'

Rufus wanted to say 'Right on', but checked himself. He didn't want to sound trivial, and besides he felt that this was no time for small talk. He had been in the Red House long enough for one day.

'Listen, Zala. I came to get my birth certificate. You think you could help me out?'

'What happen? You are applying for a passport to do some travelling?'

'I want to go to the States to study.'

'Don't go to Brooklyn,' Zala warned. 'Too much rat and cockroach. Go to Atlanta. Atlanta in Georgia. Atlanta is like the black capital.'

Rufus saw the question of the birth certificate receding into the distance, and tried to bring it back into prominence.

'I need to get the birth certificate before they will give me a passport to travel.'

'I could take care of that, man. No problem. You could get it by Friday morning.'

'You see the same damn thing! You see the same damn blasted thing! Why the hell you don't get my title-deed by Friday

19

morning, too? That land is my land. Why you don't want to give me my deed?'

It was the roving protester. She had heard everything and she had heard enough. She anchored herself to the counter between Rufus and Zala, and continued to command the attention of all and sundry with her shouting. Everyone was treated to the details about the property in Sans Souci left to her in her great-aunt's will, about how an estate-owner in the area had stolen the land and fenced it off, and about how the Government was protecting the thief and hiding the deed from her, the rightful owner. It was clear that Zala and the other clerks knew who she was and what she wanted. No one else spoke; no one moved. But during a momentary lull in her tirade, Zala made so bold as to say:

'Lady, you at the wrong counter, you know.'

'Wrong counter, my foot! Wrong counter, my backside!'

The retort resonated under the rotunda of the Red House. None the less, she did move on instantly. She did not storm out, though. She seemed to be in a thoughtful mood as she left, looking as if she felt she had got satisfaction from the clerks.

Zala winked at Rufus and remarked:

'We really have a lot of crazy people in this country.'

Rufus surrendered the application form – with some of the spaces unfilled – and excused himself, promising Zala that they would have 'a good ole talk one of these good days'.

Seeing Pinhead had irritated him. For all his political activism, Pinhead had been a class clown. In a sense, he and Rufus had been rival clowns at school, each excelling in his particular style. Rufus used to relish corny jokes, forced puns and other types of word games. He amused the fifth form and was put in detention by the English teacher for his personal considerations on Lady

Macbeth's 'Unsex me now'. Pinhead had been more of a heckler, a master in the art of what the boys called 'fatigue'. He showed no mercy with his wisecracks, picking on those who had something to hide – Bertrand, for instance. At the market early one Saturday morning, he had glimpsed Bertrand ducking for cover behind some boxes. Deducing that the fish vendor was Bertrand's mother, he had addressed her by name:

'How much a pound for the kingfish, Mrs Johnson?'

'How come you know my name?' she had asked.

'I am a very good friend of your son Bertrand,' he had replied.

The following Monday morning, Bertrand was the target of much taunting from Pinhead, who claimed that he was bringing up the subject only because Bertrand had hidden behind the boxes.

'When I go to the market I like to know the people I am buying from, because I don't like to buy from strangers. And a man like Bertrand who has such a good sense for fish pretended he didn't even see me. He went and hid behind a big box. Or maybe he just had to bend down to pick up a fish that fell down on the ground. Because I can't believe my good friend would be hiding from me. I had to introduce myself to his queen, when he should have been there to do the honours.'

The other boys had joined in, and even Rufus, much to his own surprise, had found himself saying:

'This whole thing smells very fishy for a man who has such a good sense for fish. I always thought he had a scent of fish.'

From then on, all the boys called Bertrand 'Fishy', and in time he overcame his embarrassment and took pride in his nickname.

But even though Rufus had laughed and contributed, he didn't approve. In the first place, he felt vulnerable because his own Auntie Mavis might easily have been mistaken for a fish vendor, from the way she would haggle over prices and gut fish in full view of the public at Blanchisseuse. He felt vulnerable for another reason. It wasn't just the fact of his so-called illegitimate birth. That would not have been in itself a cause for fatigue; it was too commonplace a fact of life. It needed to be accompanied by some more juicy element of scandal before even Pinhead would condescend to bring it into his repertoire. Rufus sensed there were many such elements in the circumstances of his birth, though he couldn't tell precisely what they were. But the whole business of his mother's disappearance would certainly have provided substance for Pinhead's unkind routine; hence his irritation on meeting Pinhead – now Zala – after all these years, at the Red House, the forbidding repository of recorded information.

Zala was true to his word, and set about the task of obtaining Rufus's birth certificate with uncharacteristic energy. It wasn't his fault that he had only disappointing news for Rufus on Friday morning.

'You sure your name is Rufus Linton?' Zala asked him.

Rufus wasn't prepared for this, but he was willing to accept it as another of the old Pinhead's jokes.

'Boy, you will never change, eh? Same old Pinhead. Can't take nothing seriously, except revolution.'

Zala was proud that his reputation lived on in the memory of the rival clown.

'This ain't no joke, man. I am asking you a serious question.'

'Well, if you really want to know, I am still carrying my slave name. Maybe one day I'll get liberated like you.'

Zala didn't like the tone of that, but he tried again.

'Look, the whole point is that they don't have any birth certificate made out for any Rufus Linton, except one who was born some time back in 1907, and that can't be you. If this wasn't for you, I would have given up this search long time already. You know how many people I send back home to get all the facts right when one little thing wrong on the application form?'

There was no getting away from it, no getting away from a little conference with his Auntie Mavis. As she had returned from the pre-dawn mass in a bad mood, he thought it best to wait till evening.

Mavis Linton was a highly successful businesswoman. She had been the first in the Linton family to go to university, after outstanding performances at Bishop Anstey High School in Port-of-Spain. At the University of Bristol she had studied Economics. Armed with her first-class honours degree and supported by the influence of her well-known father (the Reverend Linton), she had immediately been appointed to a prestigious and well-paid job in the civil service. Within five years she headed the Scarborough department. Advancing any higher meant moving to Trinidad, a move she welcomed as a tribute and challenge to her talent, disregarding her mother's protests that, by her education, drive and accomplishments, she was taking herself out of the marriage market.

In England she used to be mistaken for someone from the Middle East or Ethiopia, and in Trinidad she was described as 'French Creole' or 'red'. By European, Middle Eastern or African standards, she had winsome looks, with eyebrows so perfectly formed that at school she had been falsely accused of using eyebrow pencil. The mobility of her features enabled her, through inspired artistry or consummate empathy, to have a facial expression to match every situation. When, as often happened, neighbours came into her kitchen to tell her their tales of woe, she looked as careworn as they. Yet her face, in repose, retained no hint of worry, all trace of wrinkles being banished from her brow. Not a wrinkle, not a crease, not a furrow blemished her ageless face framed in close-cropped hair of solid grey. Through an unfortunate combination of improper care and bad dentistry, she had worn dentures since her mid-thirties, but she was not afraid to smile.

And how she used to beam when Rufus made her proud in front of her friends, when she played any note on the piano, and he could identify it without looking, when he entertained and impressed her visitors by spelling 'obstetrician', 'ophthalmology', 'simultaneity', 'incandescent', 'trinitrotoluene', long words, obscure words, difficult words, words he and everyone else mispronounced, words he didn't know the meaning of. She spurned no opportunity to show off his talents through the solo spelling-bee and the musical parlour game. Recognizing him for the musical prodigy he was, she taught him as much as she knew about playing the piano, after which she paid for seven years of piano lessons and monitored his stupendous progress. He then started saying he wanted to learn to play the steelband. There she withheld encouragement, unable to bring herself to look at a discarded oil drum and see a musical instrument. He dropped out of piano lessons, noticing that whenever he said 'I really want to learn to beat pan', she didn't beam.

To look at her face was to look at strength blended with a welcoming compassion, in response to which petitioners were constantly seeking her out for an audience, in order to discuss questions weighty and trivial. Some wanted advice or a sympathetic ear; some just wanted to gossip or while away the time; some wanted character references or recommendations; some wanted help in drafting personal or official letters. Truly Auntie Mavis was born to listen and counsel. Had she wanted to make money, she could have charged for consultancy services. She was not one to be inquisitorial; she was not one to probe; she would wait to be told. She had the ability to divide her attention between the words being addressed to her and her own private thoughts on other matters. Her questions and comments, however, made it clear that she was following closely what was being said to her. She held open kitchen on Saturday and open dining-room on Sunday. Because his nose was often in a book, Rufus was an invisible pair of ears; when the confidential nature of the discussion heightened his visibility and prompted his expulsion from the room, he would continue to absorb the conversation from elsewhere in the house.

By its very design and construction, Auntie Mavis's house invited quiet eavesdropping and surveillance. Unlike the more modern-looking houses on the street, with glass louvres or glass panes, the house had the old-fashioned jalousies that met the first requirement for discreet observation: when the slats were closed, Rufus had the distinct advantage of being able to see outside without being seen. Then there were the ventilation slats at the top of every wall, every partition, every door frame. They encouraged the air to circulate, and where it circulated, so did dust, mosquitoes, flies and voices – including those originating next door. Since in a real sense the walls had ears, it would have been objectivity verging on callousness to call Rufus a snoop. Without making any attempt to listen, he couldn't avoid hearing. Even on the odd occasion when Auntie Mavis and her visitors spoke in whispers, their whispered utterances carried through the ventilation slats at the top of the walls and door frames.

What a social education, what an education in the ways of the world was imparted to him in this fashion! Marital discord, financial problems, health matters, suspected pregnancies, unwanted pregnancies, plain ole gossip of news-carrying, rumour-spreading, trouble-making *macommères* – Rufus heard it all in that house. In this way, too, he picked up fragments of information about himself; yet he heard nothing about his parentage and nothing about his birth – except once: in the days following the devastating passage of hurricane Flora through Tobago in 1963, when all other topics of discussion were displaced, Auntie Mavis confided to a visitor that Flora had brought back memories of the night Rufus was born, during hurricane Janet. It was a rare mention indeed, and he never overheard any further details of his birth. There were, however, innumerable intriguing details to overhear regarding other people.

Who could say how much credence Auntie Mavis lent to some of the reports brought to her? Was it true that the little boy living two houses to the left had been fathered by a priest? Was it true that the shop-keeper at the corner had accumulated his wealth by making a pact with the devil? Rufus, to be on the safe side, denied no one the benefit of the doubt, and believed everything.

In much the same way as he acquired that social education, he received a great part of his early political education by simply keeping his ears open while lying on his bed. For example, he found out about a feud between Dr Eric Williams and somebody called C.L.R. when he overheard a lively discussion between Auntie Mavis and some visitors. At the time, Rufus was very preoccupied with his studies, as he was preparing for the 11-plus examinations. But he was aware of the labour unrest in some parts of Trinidad. There were strikes in the sugar-cane areas, amid much talk about conspiracies and subversion. He therefore pricked up his ears when one of the visitors contended that Dr Williams was ungrateful, because C.L.R. had been like a father to him.

'Like a father and a teacher. Can you imagine that? Whenever he had any problems up in Oxford, it was C.L.R. who used to help him out. And now look at how Eric turned on him and locked him up in his own house. The man came down here to report on cricket, and Eric put him under house arrest. You really never know who to trust or who is your friend these days, I tell you.'

Auntie Mavis jumped to the defence of her idol:

'Dr Williams is not a spiteful man. He had to do it for the sake of the country. He can't let anybody destroy this country, not even his own father. He loves this country more than any C.L.R.'

'I think Eric is only jealous of C.L.R.'s brains,' another visitor said. 'You know they say C.L.R. is the brightest man in the world, and Eric is only the third brightest.'

'That is a whole heap of nonsense,' Auntie Mavis protested. 'Eric Williams got a BA with first class honours from Oxford. He was first in the first class. Did C.L.R. do that? And if C.L.R. were the brightest man in the world, he wouldn't be a Communist. He wouldn't be so stupid, he would be smarter than that.'

Rufus put his books aside, got off the bed and went to re-examine the picture of Dr Williams that Auntie Mavis displayed on her bureau, beside a statue of the Virgin holding the infant Jesus. Dr Williams's head was turned slightly to the left, suggesting that the photographer might have wished to show the hearing-aid in the right ear. The dark glasses he was wearing prevented Rufus from telling whether the hint of a smile on his face was the type of smile Auntie Mavis would describe as one coming from the eyes and the heart, or the type she would dismiss as a copy of a smile contrived in a show of teeth. His mouth was not open. What the exceptionally intelligent half-smile confirmed to Rufus was that the man in the picture was unquestionably one of the brightest men in the world. He understood why Auntie Mavis, a staunch Catholic, wanted him to gain admission to Dr Williams's Alma Mater instead of the secondary school run by Catholic priests.

Rufus was both proud and intimidated not only to have been born in the country that had produced two of the three brainiest men in the world, but also to be aspiring to enter Queen's Royal College, which they had attended. What a challenge! In a country with such an abundance of brain, would he be able to do well enough in the competitive examinations to secure a place at the college that was his first choice?

He was intrigued and fascinated, too. Auntie Mavis often spoke about Dr Williams, but he had never heard her mention this C.L.R. When the visitors left and he plied her with questions about him, she was grudging in her admiration.

'His name is C.L.R. James,' she said. 'He is very bright, but not brilliant like Dr Williams. A couple of years ago, he wrote a book called *Beyond a Boundary*. He praises his brains a lot, but it's a good book. You must read it one day.'

Almost as an afterthought, she added: 'I will tell you one thing though: if it hadn't been for C.L.R. they would never have made Worrell captain. Never!'

Seldom did she speak about cricket. Unlike her brother Clive, she was no cricket fan; netball was her game. In her heyday, her height had served her well and had made her the designated 'shoot' in many a netball tournament. She had even travelled up the islands on a Trinidad and Tobago team for an inter-territorial championship. Only a liar would have said that she failed to carry her lithe six-foot frame with elegance, yet people often blamed her height for the fact that she had never married. As to whether she cared about that, no one could easily tell. It was a question she never discussed with anyone, not even her closest friends. She was extremely busy. After being lured away from the Ministry of Finance to a position at a commercial bank, she continued to excel. She was a hard worker, but consistently refused to work overtime or on weekends. 'I put in an honest day's work, five days a week. I need the leisure time to be with the family,' was the way she explained it, prompting only token noises of disapproval from her colleagues, who realized that in her 'honest day's work' she produced far more than those who liked it to be known that they worked long hours overtime.

She always said 'the family', but would have been more accurate saying 'my family', which was what, in her heart of hearts, she considered Rufus, Pearl and Tony to be. To Rufus, Auntie Mavis was undoubtedly the most kind-hearted person in the world. She was the one who had volunteered to take total charge of the children her brothers had fathered out of wedlock, Pearl (Cecil's daughter), Tony (Graham's son) and, the youngest of the lot, Rufus.

Even though Tony no longer lived with her, Auntie Mavis was just as worried as before about him. He had been showing her disrespect before he had even entered his teens, and she had never liked the company he kept with people living 'behind the bridge'. The example of schoolchildren whose limbs had been severed by the wheels of the train might have been a warning to others, but not to Tony. Despite his own near escapes, he would hop on and off the train without fear of slipping, simply for the fun of it. At Auntie Mavis's suggestion, he had reluctantly become an altar boy. She had hoped that the routine, the discipline, the proximity to the sacred mysteries would help to keep him on the straight and narrow, and give some direction to his life. After two uneventful months of serving at the altar, Tony was caught by the sexton red-handed, drinking the sacramental wine. Instead of humbling himself and promising never to do it again, he charged that most of the altar boys and the parish priest himself regularly helped themselves to the wine.

'I was only doing what I learned from them,' he told the sexton, who duly reported all the details to the priest.

After being dismissed, Tony vowed never to set foot in any church again. He was true to his word and was the only member of the household missing when Rufus made his First Communion. He must have been extremely drunk or totally under the influence of his girlfriend to go to the 5 o'clock mass at which he disgraced his aunt.

Auntie Mavis had long been assailed by doubts as to whether she had done her best when she had had him under her charge. As an adolescent living in her house, he had undermined her confidence in her ability to keep him out of trouble. He had grown more and more sullen, barely speaking to her, and avoiding looking at her on the rare occasions when he did speak. She had always tried not to reproach her brothers for their irresponsibility and their lack of interest in the children they had fathered out of wedlock. But now she had no hesitation in blaming her brother Graham for the way Tony was turning out. Having seen him descend from his exalted position at the altar to the floor at the back of the church, she was fearful that he might end up in the gutters of Port-of-Spain.

Rufus, on the other hand, would go far. In her eyes, he was a completely different individual and had no difficulty in communicating with her. She was therefore surprised and hurt – and Rufus felt shame and contrition – that he had told her nothing about his plans, at least not in the recent past. She hadn't expected him to continue teaching at the College indefinitely; when he was repeating his A Levels, he had discussed with her his ambition to go to university and his hopes of winning a scholarship. But now that he had settled into his job at the College after teaching there for a full year, he had given her no sign that he was thinking of leaving. She didn't know that he was still planning to go abroad.

For his A Levels, he had wanted to offer English, French and History, with the intention of doing a degree in English, but Auntie Mavis and others advised him that if he studied something practical and marketable like Economics, he would easily land a good job at the World Bank or the United Nations. He therefore opted for Economics instead of French. The first time he took the examinations, he got an A in English, and B's in History and Economics; the second time, he got A's in English and Economics, and a C in History. On both occasions, there was such stiff competition for the few scholarships offered by the Government that he failed in his bid.

It wasn't for lack of application. In preparing for the examinations, he had exhibited a single-mindedness Auntie Mavis couldn't remember seeing since the days when he had had his dog Twinkle to look after – making sure the matches, candles and oil lamps on the dresser were at the ready, forcing himself to go to sleep at 8 o'clock, studying assiduously from 3 in the morning, power cut or no power cut. How Rufus rued his fate! And how he envied the lucky few scholarship winners who, in their published interviews, happily discussed their travel and study plans! His grades were sure to qualify him for the overseas university of his choice, but they were not good enough for a scholarship, and without a scholarship, he couldn't afford to go.

'Then why don't you apply to St Augustine?' Auntie Mavis suggested. 'We can afford that.'

Rufus had heard of scholarships being awarded by the bank where she worked. He wondered why she didn't ask for a scholarship for him.

'It would be good for me to see the outside world,' he replied. 'I will try to get a job at the College and save for a couple of years.'

Having pinned his hopes on Rufus to bring glory to the College by winning one of the coveted scholarships, the principal of the College shared his disappointment that a school in San Fernando had again run off with the honours. He was only too happy to have Rufus back as an English master while he saved up for university, and soon he became a sort of mentor to Rufus, giving him detailed advice on university admission procedures and on life in England – even though Rufus had told him more than once that he was more interested in going to the United States.

That was another thing that made Rufus feel shame and contrition: the fact that his lifelong confidante, with whom he had shared problems far more private and secret, had been left in the dark about a matter that he had discussed openly with members of the staff of the College other than the principal, a matter, therefore, that was not even confidential. He couldn't explain it to himself; all he knew was that, on more than one occasion, he had been on the point of broaching the subject and had been prevented, either because she had said something that had made it slip out of his mind, or because for some other reason, he had decided that it was not the right time. It was as if mischievous forces had conspired to create the impression of secrecy where no cause for secrecy existed. And now it was too late to rescue the situation.

'I've been minding you all your life like my own child, and you were making plans to go away and keeping them from me. You think that is nice?' said Auntie Mavis.

'I didn't mean it that way, Tantie. I wasn't going to run away, you know. I just wasn't ready to tell everybody as yet.'

'Everybody! But I am not everybody. I do more for you than your own mother.'

Rufus was silent. He resented being reminded.

'And besides,' Auntie Mavis continued, 'you don't even need a birth certificate to get the passport.'

'They told me at the Passport Office I had to have the birth paper.'

'Yes, that's the rule, but I could arrange for you to get a passport in two twos even without your birth certificate.'

The offer came as a surprise to Rufus. Mavis Linton was vocal in her condemnation of anything resembling queue-jumping and use of influence. She was particularly reluctant to use her position and contacts to advance the interests of relatives or friends, preferring to help out total strangers who she felt had greatest need of her protection. It was an open secret that when Rufus was permitted to take the 11-plus examinations at the age of nine, she had intervened on his behalf to have the rules bent. But that was only because common sense had so dictated; it was obvious to her that her child prodigy of a nephew would be frustrated for life if held back and forced to mark time.

Mindful of her reputation as the patron of the unknown underdog, Rufus now commented:

'But I thought you say you not pulling strings for none of your family.'

Auntie Mavis's face betrayed irritation, not so much at what Rufus had said as at how he had said it – in the style and intonation of the local parlance. She never grew tired of correcting other people's pronunciation and syntax, and if the matter at hand had not demanded such thoughtful consideration, she might have asked him to rephrase his remark. Instead, she said simply:

'I could make an exception since you're so anxious to get your passport.'

'Tantie, is true I want to get my passport. But you don't find it strange that they can't find my birth certificate under my name?'

'Forget about the birth certificate. You don't need it.'

Rufus didn't forget about the birth certificate. He brooded over it for the remainder of the evening, constantly haunted by Zala's question: 'You sure your name is Rufus Linton?' In the process, he decided on a line of investigation which he hoped would not provoke in his aunt the irritation and reticence he remembered from the days when he used to ask about his mother.

'Tantie,' he said casually on Monday evening. 'You know Rose MacSween had to go through a whole lot of trouble to get her name changed.'

'So she too went and adopted one of those strange-sounding so-called African names. Nobody even knows what they mean.'

'You think anybody in Trinidad knows what Elizabeth or Margaret or Carol or even my name Rufus means?'

'But at least those names don't sound as savage as Zankula and Potowewe.'

'People find they sound strange because they are brain-washed,' Rufus argued. 'It's time to unwash a few brains in this country.'

Rufus was pleased with the way the conversation was going. Life had already taught him that it was sometimes better not to get to the point too soon. He continued:

'You know they have some priests in this country who are refusing to christen children because the parents want to give them African names.'

'The priests are doing the children a favour. With those strange-sounding savage names, everybody would laugh at them in school.'

'I don't really find the names sound so strange or savage, you know. A fellow I went to school with changed his name to Zala. You find that sounds strange and savage?'

'He's lucky he didn't have that name when he was in school,' Auntie Mavis persisted. 'They would have found some way to torment him. He would have begged his parents to give him a nice name.'

'What you mean is an English name, like Robert or Charles.'

'No, it doesn't have to be an English name, you know. It could be a Spanish name – like Roberto or Carlos. Don't you find those names sound nice?'

Auntie Mavis chuckled, pretending to stare at the clock on the wall while observing Rufus out of the corner of her eye to see if he got the joke. Rufus obliged her with an exaggerated snort of fake amusement.

'Four-knee,' he said, not the least bit embarrassed by his corniness, and touching his knee to emphasize the second syllable. 'Hi, Lee, four-knee.'

'What your generation needs is a sense of humour. One day I'm going to write a book about the lack of sense of humour in the young generation,' Auntie Mavis warned him.

Rufus broke the ensuing silence with another of his studied casual remarks:

'Anyway, Rose didn't change her name to an African name.'

'Oh God, don't tell me they have gone into Carib names now. Her mother always used to say they had some Carib blood in them, as if cannibal blood was some mark of distinction.'

'It's only their enemies they used to eat, and it was only to punish them, not because they were hungry. Anytime a Carib was hungry, all he had to do was go in the forest and kill a wild animal.'

'I spent money for you to go to school to learn that kind of nonsense, Rufus?' said Auntie Mavis, trying to sound indignant, but thoroughly enjoying what she thought of as a heart-to-heart with her favourite nephew. The ensuing silence was for the second time broken by Rufus:

'Anyway, Rose didn't change her name to an African name or a Carib name either. She just wanted to have the name Rose as her official name. On her birth certificate, all they had was "Prudence MacSween", although nobody ever called her "Prudence" and everybody always called her "Rose". Now she wants to be Rose Prudence or maybe Prudence Rose, two very nice and proper-sounding names.'

'At least they sound better than Karakwe Batatsu,' admitted Auntie Mavis, who hated the name Prudence.

Rufus having by now assumed a deeply pensive look, Auntie Mavis at once saw what was coming, and silently reproached herself. How could she, with her broad experience of deviousness, have allowed herself to be trapped so easily? She did feel admiration though, and pride. Rufus was clever. Oh yes, she had always known that Rufus was clever. At one point, she had even thought that he might be a prodigy. But now he had proved himself to be devious, and deviousness, like a sense of humour, was an attribute she would have liked to see more in evidence among the younger generation. She didn't hurry him. She let him break the silence for the third time, in his own time.

'You know something I was just studying, Auntie Mavis?'

'What?'

'Suppose when they went to register my birth, they gave one name, and then at home everybody started to call me by a different name. Maybe that is why they can't find my birth certificate. I was just wondering if something happened like with Rose – if Rufus is just my home name and they have another name on my birth certificate. Maybe that is why they can't find the certificate.'

Auntie Mavis was silent for a full five minutes. She realized she could no longer stall Rufus, could no longer conceal the fact which he had obviously managed to divine. She would have preferred to consult her mother first, but Mrs Judith Linton had, for the umpteenth time, turned her back on Trinidad and retired to Tobago, where she couldn't be reached immediately. Auntie Mavis, however, was used to taking major decisions without consulting anyone, and she startled Rufus with the brief and direct assertion:

'The name on your birth certificate is "Prince Linton".'

Rufus still had one week of vacation before the second term began, but he couldn't bring himself to return to the Red House so soon. Was it a lack of courage to face Zala or just the usual procrastination syndrome? It had been his intention to leave Trinidad by September 1975. Since the close of the 1973–1974 school year, he had been meaning to start getting information on colleges and universities in the United States, finding out about admission requirements and application procedures, and looking into the question of financial assistance. He knew he would also have to apply for a student visa, but would first need a passport. Indolence had set in, but just before the Christmas break, he had begun to panic. It was at an end-of-term party that he had shared with the principal of the College his alarm at the flight of time and his failure to attend to those various matters; he intimated that he might be needing some time off during the second term. Years ago, the principal had discovered that invariably the teaching schedule was disrupted when staff took time off. Understandably, he was loath to make exceptions to his strict policy even for Rufus. It was agreed, however, that if Rufus couldn't do otherwise, he might leave school during class time, but only when he had no teaching assignments. As it happened, he had nothing but free periods after lunch on Wednesdays, so on the first Wednesday afternoon of the new term, Rufus made his third visit to the Red House.

The rainy season wasn't supposed to start until May. But whatever the local almanac might have said, the drenching rain that had been coming down during the greater part of the morning was bound to continue for at least another three or four hours. Rufus knew he wasn't mistaken about that! He had barely run down the steps from the staff room before his shirt was clinging to his back. When the taxi that stopped for him moved off, he did his best to squeeze himself against the door so as not to dampen the clothing of the passenger in the middle of the back seat. All the way to the Red House, the vehicle wheezed as it ploughed through the flooded streets, splashing water over the reckless few who were not huddled under the overhanging balconies, the impatient few who were not waiting for the sun to come blazing down again.

Pedestrian traffic along the pathway through the Red House between St Vincent and Abercromby Streets had come to a standstill. The area under the dome of the building was heavily congested with people waiting for the rain to stop. Some were studying the notice-boards as if they were there for that very purpose, others were chatting and milling about without pretence. Rufus couldn't tell who was supposed to be at work in the Red House, who was waiting to be attended to, and who was simply sheltering. Indeed he might have despaired of ever locating Zala, had he not heard his name from the latter's mouth. Misled by a confusing echo, Rufus initially looked in the wrong direction, but his ears having made a quick adjustment, he turned to see the selfsame Zala standing by a notice-board and beckoning. At the approach of his sodden friend, Zala couldn't resist a bit of playful scolding:

'Boy, you don't know about sheltering from the rain? You smelling like canal water! You need to change all your clothes! Why you went through the rain? You looking for death from pneumonia or what? You don't want to go away again?'

Not a hint of smugness was to be detected in Zala, however. He had been right in his conjecture that 'Rufus' was not the name under which his friend's birth had been declared, but, to Rufus's immense relief, he had long since outgrown the penchant for gloating. He was just as talkative and willing to help as he had been during Rufus's two previous visits.

'No sweat,' he assured Rufus. 'If you know how many people don't even know what name on their birth certificate. Come back in a week's time.'

It was with an ineffable sense of achievement that Rufus took possession of his birth certificate the following Wednesday afternoon. He immediately folded it and headed for a café on St Vincent Street, securely holding on to the written confirmation of his official identity. To prepare himself for his first look at it, he bought himself a beer, took a full half-hour to finish it, and, again passing through the Red House, walked up to the fountain in the middle of Woodford Square. He gathered from an inscription that the fountain had been presented to the Borough of Port-of-Spain by Gregor Turnbull of Glasgow in 1866. These days, the fountain was even drier than the river not too far away that was known as the 'Dry River', but Rufus remembered when it used to be a water fountain in the true sense of the term, like the night Auntie Mavis took him to a massive political rally in the Square and enthusiastically pointed out Dr Eric Williams – 'The Chancellor of this University of Woodford Square,' she said. Though she neglected to add 'and the brightest man in the world', he knew that she discounted all the talk from others about C.L.R. James being the brightest and Eric only the third brightest. Yet he had never heard her or anyone else say who the second brightest man in the world was.

Rufus sat on a bench near the fountain, and for a long time he remained staring at the over-ripe berries that had fallen to the ground. He then walked to the eastern end of the Square and listened to a man expostulating with a few stragglers on the merits of wife-beating and the inequities of the criminal justice system. He didn't have much of an audience. A couple of yards away, however, a larger group had formed round a man lecturing on nutrition:

'The reason the children today getting duncier and duncier is because their parents don't give them the right food. That is why they can't learn. That is why they having to wear glasses and going crazy at such an early age. Some of them clean crazy. Some of them dirty crazy. They eating too much fry chicken. They not eating ground provisions and vegetables and nuts. Take example from the gorilla. A gorilla will eat nuts all day. And look at the gorilla. A gorilla is the strongest person.'

Another debater intervened:

'The children not duncey at all. The children bright. You didn't hear what Dr Williams say? You know I find we have a lotta pretensive people in this country. All you people too ungrateful. You know why the Doctor always turning off his hearing aid? In order not to hear ungrateful people like all you. Or maybe you just plain cantankerous, ignorant and forgetful. Before Dr Williams, you had to be white or to be some kind of somebody in this country before your child could go to Convent. Now every Tom, Dick and Harry going to Convent since Dr Williams bring universal education. That man really believes in education. I remember when I was in Standard Five, I was doing my homework about imports and exports. And I was catching my tail, because I couldn't find the information. So my mother tell me to ring up Dr Williams. So we went by the neighbour next door to use the telephone and ring up Dr Williams. I will never forget this. Dr Williams say to me: "Little boy, can you write down big numbers?" And I say: "Yes, thanks, Doctor." And out of his head he give me all the figures about imports and exports. And that is how I got to do my homework. Now, you think they could ever get me to vote for anybody else while I'm still alive? Never happen!'

That one would get along well with Auntie Mavis, Rufus thought, as he walked back to the bench to continue staring at the berries.

He didn't care for the name Prince, and was glad that the habitual tormentors at school had not known him by that name. But it was as Auntie Mavis had said: under the heading 'Name (if any)', was written 'Prince Linton'. Directly below was written 'Illegitimate'. That word offended Rufus, without, however, causing him any sense of shame. He remembered the day at school when he had written an essay entitled 'The ills of society'. He had dealt at length with the question of the unfair treatment accorded to those branded as 'illegitimate' by society, and, true to form, he had ended with a play on words which the teacher had proudly read out to the class:

'In the final analysis, no so-called illegitimate child conceives of himself as illegitimate. The illegitimate conception is that of his parents.'

And now here it was in black and white, the description of himself which he felt more properly applied to his parents and therefore should be on some official record of their identity. On an impulse, he changed the wording on the certificate to read 'Of illegitimate parents'. Thus amusing himself, he burst out laughing, causing a passer-by to shake his head in commiseration with so young a man going crazy.

Because the whole question of the 'illegitimate' label was so important to Rufus, he had lingered on that column. He now moved on to the columns about his parents. At first he was convinced that there had to be some mistake. The column concerning his father was blank, except for a dash, which was apparently supposed to mean that no information was available. But how could that be? He knew who his father was. Everybody, for that matter, knew who his father was. And Clive Linton had never denied that Rufus was his son, at least not within Rufus's hearing. So why should all information about his father, even his name, have been withheld? It was in pondering these questions that he was startled to find, staring up at him from the birth certificate, the answer to a question he had actually asked. Name of mother: Miss Linton. This answer, however, served only to confuse Rufus and prompt further vexing questions. How could his mother's name possibly be Miss Linton? How could his father be Clive and his mother a Miss Linton? Linda had long been married, Carmen had got married some time after he was born, and Mavis had never been married. Who could this Miss Linton be? Surely not Carmen. And surely not Mavis. Or could she? Was she? Impossible. Clive Linton was his father. Mavis was Clive's sister. He simply could not seriously entertain the idea that he could be the product of an incestuous union. He would have known by now. People would have talked. He would have heard something. He might even have been shunned. He would have been made to pay dearly for that sin of his parents. No, he concluded, Mavis Linton was not his mother. But to get her views on the matter and some answers to the other questions now raised by his birth certificate, he decided to have another talk with Auntie Mavis.

She was not unprepared for this fact-finding session; she had been expecting it ever since she had made the brief and direct assertion to Rufus about his official name. She was not going to let Rufus beat about the bush this time, but it was immediately clear that he had no inclination to beat about any bush.

'How come Uncle Clive name not on my birth certificate as my father?' he began.

'That is a question you will have to ask Uncle Clive,' she answered.

Rufus had for years thought of Clive Linton as 'Uncle Clive'. The idea that he should so refer to Clive had been suggested by the latter's mother, who had argued that it would be 'unseemly and improper' for Rufus to be encouraged to address or refer to Clive as 'Daddy', like the children Clive had fathered in wedlock.

'Sheila will not like it,' she had said, priding herself on her sensitivity and attentiveness to the wishes of her daughter-in-law.

Clive had waited to disclose the existence of Rufus until some time after his marriage to Sheila. At first, she had persuaded herself that Rufus was of little consequence, given the solidity and apparent durability of the sentiment that now linked her to Clive. She had anxiously awaited the birth of her first child, whom she had envisaged as an all-important counterweight to Rufus. Even after the fifth child, however, she had still looked apprehensively for signs that Clive would show some partiality towards Rufus. Clive had done nothing to inspire such apprehensions. His attitude towards Rufus was one of utter indifference, which Sheila had finally interpreted as a clear indication of a decisive break with his past life. It was true, though, that Sheila would not have liked to hear Rufus call Clive 'Daddy'.

There was little danger of that happening. Rufus had had no choice but to digest the fact that 'Daddy' was not the authorized form of address. Those around him either did not notice or chose to disregard his secret retaliation: he always managed to circumvent the use of the authorized 'Uncle Clive' in directly addressing Clive Linton. Indeed, he managed to dispense with the vocative altogether. Which was not to say that he did not speak to Clive Linton; but on the rare occasions when Rufus felt absolutely obliged to use the vocative form of address, he was able to utter some indistinct mumble that could be interpreted as the listener wished.

Third-person references to Clive Linton proved to be a more intractable problem. There the pronoun 'he' was of invaluable assistance on many an occasion. Yet there were times when it clearly would not suffice. If Clive Linton, his wife and children were not within earshot, Rufus would use, as sparingly as possible, the words 'Uncle Clive'. If any or all of the above were within earshot, Rufus exercised his ingenuity, sometimes putting on a show of patently exaggerated respect in order to justify the use of 'Mr Linton', sometimes approximating disrespectful familiarity in using 'Clivey', as Clive Linton was known to his buddies. But never on such occasions would the words 'Uncle Clive' cross Rufus's lips.

Alone with Auntie Mavis, the inhibition vanished, and he now had no difficulty in using the words 'Uncle Clive', when he could so easily have said 'he':

'Uncle Clive doesn't like people to ask him questions.'

And that was the end of that fact-finding session, for Auntie Mavis said nothing, Rufus cracked his fingers, thought he would ask another question, changed his mind, and pondered his next move.

Tobago

On Friday afternoon, right after school, Rufus was on his way to Piarco to catch a plane to Tobago. He had said a special prayer to Saint Christopher for safe passage, but he remained exceedingly tense. He had never been on a plane before, having taken the overnight boat on every previous visit to Tobago. As the plane climbed, though, his apprehension was eclipsed by his fascination with the densely forested undulations of the Northern Range. For a moment, he thought he was looking at Cerro Aripo, the highest peak on the island. Or maybe it was El Tucuche, the second highest – or maybe neither, maybe just some minor hill whose name he would not recognize, maybe just some minor hill which the Spaniards had omitted to name. Cerro Aripo, El Tucuche, El Tucuche, Cerro Aripo, Cerro Aripo, El Tucuche ... There was poetic majesty in the incantation that resounded in his brain like a mantra being recited, bringing back other names that had always produced a mesmerizing chant in his head, names like Nanda Devi, Cotopaxi and Krakatoa. Placed beside Krakatoa, his own Cerro Aripo and El Tucuche at just over 3,000 feet could hold their own, but they would have been dwarfed by Cotopaxi and Nanda Devi. Trinidad's Northern Range would have passed unnoticed among the lowly foothills of the Himalayas.

He tried and failed to imagine what it might be like to fly between Nepal and Tibet over the Himalayas. The Himalayas were an abstraction in a geography book. Mount Everest itself was an abstraction. The Northern Range, on the other hand, had been a concrete and vital point of reference ever since he had become aware of his surroundings. He was confident he could never be completely lost. He had only to locate the Northern Range in order to tell which way was north. In his present state of anxiety, he was comforted and exhilarated by the knowledge that the Northern Range was below him. He could look down upon it and see how its slopes were blemished by brownish scars, and wonder whether the palettes of the world's finest painters could be equal to the task of capturing its whole spectrum of browns and greens.

When he looked out of the window again, the Northern Range was gone. He regretted his inattention, for he had intended to try and pinpoint from the plane the secluded beach on the north coast that had become his favourite, or the fish market where Auntie Mavis used to gut fish. Ah well, he would try on the flight back. In the meantime, he made the unnerving observation that he was only a couple of hundred feet above the waves. Less than a quarter of an hour had elapsed since the plane had taken off, and already it had descended to the point where he could see fish among the algae – but no runway. His fresh prayer to Saint Christopher was interrupted by the bump that told him the flight was over, on land, not in the sea.

Though back on terra firma, Rufus was limp with trepidation. His anxiety about air travel had given way to misgivings about the wisdom of his weekend venture to Tobago, now that the encounter with his grandmother, Mrs Judith Linton, loomed ever closer.

It was at the impressionable age of 18 that Judith Fuller had made the acquaintance of the Reverend Andrew Linton. Born in Yorkshire, England, he had grown up in a very Catholic family, and had always wanted to become a priest. While preparing for the priesthood, he had inexplicably given up. Some said it was because he was having trouble with all the Latin. In any event, he had become an Anglican and had eventually fulfilled his vocation. Long afflicted by asthma, he had yielded to the seductive prospect of warm, sunny climes in seizing the opportunity to go to Tobago in 1927. As head-master of the Anglican School in Scarborough, he had appointed Judith Fuller to his teaching staff in 1928.

Their marriage the following year prompted the use of such phrases as 'a match made in heaven', delighting the hearts and kindling the hopes of the mothers of marriageable daughters, whose minds joined in prayer for the arrival of other marriageable ministers from the mother country. The Lintons were a prolific couple – Mavis in 1930, Linda in 1931, Clive in 1933, Cecil in 1935, and Graham in 1937. Then, almost as an afterthought, Carmen followed in 1941. In 1969, while on a visit to Trinidad, the Reverend Andrew Linton was killed in a road accident.

For a number of nights before the accident, Mrs Judith Linton had been having bad dreams, and she warned her husband that she could sense impending disaster. He shrugged off her premonitions, telling her that whenever the Good Lord was ready to take him, he would have no choice but to go. She insisted that he shouldn't take the plane, because it was going to crash. Not being too fond of flying anyway, he took the boat. As it turned out, the plane didn't crash, and the boat didn't sink.

Perhaps under the effect of her husband's fatalistic attitude, Mrs Judith Linton accepted his death as God's will. Some months later, she received a letter from a bank in Yorkshire advising her that the Reverend Linton had left specific instructions to be followed in the event of his death: the manager was to personally see to it that Mrs Judith Linton promptly inherited her husband's savings. The remittance for several thousand pounds came as a complete surprise to her, for her husband's financial affairs had never been any of her business.

Mrs Judith Linton had long since abandoned the classroom, and with the proceeds from the Yorkshire account, now managed a guest-house not far from Mount Irvine beach. She was partial to the absentee style of management, preferring to spend most of her time in Trinidad with Linda, her favourite. More out of indifference than trust, she left the day-to-day running of the guest-house to an enthusiastic distant cousin, Dorothy. The enterprise flourished.

Having failed to notify Cousin Dorothy of his impending visit, Rufus thought he would be spared the bumpy ride in the 1953 Ford that was reserved for the most honoured guests – whether they arrived by sea or by air. But as he emerged from the airport terminal in Tobago, he was immediately spotted by Mano, the tenured driver and master mechanic attached to the 'Dulce Hogar' guest-house, who had come to meet one such honoured guest.

'Rufus man, long time no see. I thought you was dead,' said Mano, exaggeratedly tipping his trademark straw hat, and smiling at the resurrected, who returned the greeting:

'Mano man, I thought you was dead too.'

After thus establishing that they were both alive, they were able to proceed to considerations on the state of health of the 1953 Ford, until Mano remembered why he had come to the airport.

'You didn't see Mrs Adams on the plane?'

'No.'

'I suppose she change she mind.'

And off they went.

'So what brings you to Tobago, man?' Mano asked, lighting a cigarette and avoiding a pot-hole with a nonchalance that impressed Rufus.

'You still have those cancer sticks?' was Rufus's non-reply.

'Cancer ain't go kill me. I could tell you that.'

'One day this blasted old car is going to blow up on you,' Rufus assured him.

'Little boy, this car is older and wiser than you. All it need is good handling and a little servicing. The only problem is with the spare parts.'

Mano knew he was talking to someone who had little knowledge of cars, so he confined himself to those general observations. Then, for no reason that Rufus could divine, he went into a ruminative mood:

'Boy, when you see people rich, you must not envy them. You never know what they had to do to make that money. The other day in Scarborough, I watch a young fellow with a crocus bag of manure on his back walking up a hill in the hot sun 11 o'clock in the morning, selling manure from door to door. So he say to me: "Boss, you want some manure to buy?" I say to him: "No, thank you, sonny. I don't want any manure at this time." I watch the fellow and I say to myself: "You think you could find anybody else to do that work?" Now if in ten years' time, he living in a big mansion, people will turn around and wonder how he get all that money, and they will envy him and feel that he shouldn't be so rich. And they wouldn't think how he had to break his back to get where he is. Manure is not an easy thing to smell on your back.'

Rufus was still thinking about the crocus bag of manure when Mano asked again:

'But what brings you to Tobago, man?'

'I need a little rest by the sea.'

'Since when you like the sea so much? You can't even swim.'

'You ever see fish come out on land and try to walk?' Rufus inquired.

'So what would happen if you in a boat and it turn over?'

'You must teach me to swim, Mano.'

'You think I have time to teach a big old hard-back man like you to swim?'

'When I talk about your car, I am a little boy, and when I talk about swimming I am a hard-back man. But how you so?'

Mano gave a full-throated but strained laugh. He refrained from inquiring further into the motive for Rufus's visit. He settled into silent investigation of the matter, while Rufus settled into deep inhalation of the smell of the sea and equally deep contemplation of the late-evening colours. Now that the gathering dusk was reducing the glare of the sun, the ubiquitous ixora appeared more scarlet than ever. In cages that hung like decorations from the window frames of certain houses, tiny birds, some with orange bellies, some with yellow tails, fluttered about as if terrified by the coughing of the 1953 Ford. Somewhere in the roadside ditches and somewhere in the bushes, frogs had started rehearsing their call-and-response. Rufus gazed in wonder at what he thought was a woodpecker, one with a bright red crown, perched on a stunted coconut-tree. Hundreds of coconut-trees were silhouetted against the pastels, many decapitated but standing erect (they would have been perfectly serviceable as lamp-posts), others gnarled in all their ugliness. Occasionally there was a birdcage hanging from a nail on a coconut-tree.

Mano knew everybody – Curtis, Small Man, Miss Gerry, Teacher Benjie, Pundit, Skipper. He would call out a nickname or a real name as soon as he got within hailing distance, and the greeting would be acknowledged in kind. 'Hercules!' he shouted as he drove by a standpipe. Hercules had earned his sobriquet well. In his extra-tight trunks, his weightlifter physique made him the undisputed Mr Universe of the village. He hailed Mano, flashed a smile and waved with the regal gesture of a man who could picture himself in all his glory and was confident that he was genuinely a magnificent specimen. Then he resumed soaping himself at the roadside, apparently no more self-conscious or inhibited than he might have been in the privacy behind the curtain of a shower stall.

Abruptly, round a corner, the coconut plantation ended, demarcated by a mighty samaan tree that was unquestionably over a hundred years old. It had been left unscathed by Flora in 1963, and by other, more devastating hurricanes no longer within living memory. Nailed to the trunk, eight feet from the ground, was a three-foot-square wooden sign proclaiming to anyone who happened to be looking in its direction that the 'Dulce Hogar' guest-house was at hand. At the promised spot, half a mile later, the 'Dulce Hogar' guest-house came into sight, and seemed at once to belie the sign's other promise – luxury accommodation.

It must have been a delightful residence when it was built in 1947, but after years of being buffeted by the sharp blasts coming off the sea, the tarnished metalwork around it was being eaten away by the salt. The windward side had been looking particularly weather-beaten long before hurricane Flora took her toll. Until then, the structure had remained sound, for the house had been built to last. True dilapidation had set in only after it received a battering from Flora, lost its roof and suffered structural damage when a tree collapsed on it. The house was to remain unoccupied and in disrepair until Mrs Judith Linton bought it in 1970. It was an irresistible bargain. But before its faded delights could be restored, it would need a lot of work; it wasn't getting it.

The scrawny-looking hen that totally ignored the 1953 Ford was the only immediate sign of animal or human life, until Mrs Judith Linton (dressed in what she considered proper attire for the honoured and awaited Mrs Adams) stepped from inside the living-room and put on her smile of welcome – which merged with, but was not displaced by, the look of puzzlement inspired by the sight of Rufus.

'But what brings you to Tobago, Rufus boy?'

Rufus was growing tired of the question, and ignored it.

'Evening, Grannie. Auntie Mavis sent to say Good Afternoon.'

'If I had known you were coming, I would have got you to bring up some bitters for me. I can't afford the price they asking for in Tobago.'

Mrs Judith Linton had become addicted to Angostura bitters. She used it in virtually everything she ate or drank, even in coffee. She was a great believer in its therapeutic qualities, presenting herself as living proof of its effectiveness. She was seldom ill, and when the occasional 'bad feeling' came upon her, the tested and unfailing remedy consisted of four to five drops of bitters in a mug of boiling water. Her big fear was that one day the supply of the valuable medicinal product might run out. She therefore dreaded visits from her son Clive, who was a great believer in the merits of Angostura bitters in rum. 'Six dashes of bitters, and I could drink all day without getting drunk' was the boast that struck awe deep into his mother's psyche, and set her worrying about whether her best hiding-place was safe. For she had more than one hiding-place: the obvious – behind the bottles of assorted spirits at the back of the cabinet with the glass door; and what she thought of as her best hiding-place – in an old pepper-sauce bottle. The transbottling operation would be performed when no one else was around, but, unbeknown to

Mrs Judith Linton, Cousin Dorothy had discovered the secret. Delighting in sheer mischief, she would often put the pepper-sauce bottle on the table for the honoured guests – whereupon Mrs Judith Linton would hasten to remove the bottle, accusing Cousin Dorothy of trying to ruin the business by offering the guests 'that nasty stinking old bottle of pepper sauce when we have so many brand-new bottles'.

It was not surprising, then, that on seeing her grandson alight from the car in the place of the honoured, awaited Mrs Adams, Mrs Linton should at once bemoan the missed opportunity of a fresh consignment of Angostura bitters.

'I decided to come just at the last minute,' Rufus said to excuse his thoughtlessness. 'And you know how hard it is to telephone Tobago from Trinidad.'

'It hard to telephone anywhere from Trinidad,' Mrs Linton observed drily. 'But what happened to Mrs Adams?'

After dinner that night, Rufus broached the topic that had brought him to Tobago. He told her how difficult it had been to get his birth certificate at the Red House, how easy it had been once Auntie Mavis had disclosed to him his official name, how astonished he had been not to see the name of his father on the birth certificate, how reluctant Auntie Mavis had been to give him any more information. Mrs Judith Linton did not once excuse herself to go and prepare a cup of tea and Angostura bitters, and at the end of the narrative, kept shaking her head from side to side and probing her false teeth with the tip of her tongue. When she spoke, it was simply to pronounce:

'I am an old woman now, and I don't need all this bother-ation.'

Naturally, Rufus was not satisfied with this, but he could think of no way to detain his grandmother, who now departed to her room. On Sunday afternoon, as he was leaving for the airport, she said to him:

'Go and see Miss Haynes on Belmont Circular Road. Tell her I sent you.'

Belmont Circular Road

With the heaviest of hearts, Rufus took a taxi to Belmont Circular Road. When his dog Twinkle died, he had sworn never to go back to Miss Haynes's house, and he hadn't been there since. The house was an unpretentious two-bedroom dwelling whose brick walls had been plastered over some five years after construction. They had never been painted. The steel poles sticking out of the flat concrete roof suggested that the original project to erect a storied building had been abandoned. At the back of the house, there stood a mango-tree that bore fruit of the coveted 'Julie' variety. Miss Haynes would have liked to have it cut down, for it attracted into her yard the undesirable juvenile element. The hapless Little Scobie from next door was endlessly being flogged by his parents after being reported for mango-stealing by Miss Haynes. More accurately, Little Scobie had suffered only a few floggings, after which Mr Scobie began to argue with his wife, the flogger, that the boy should not be punished for helping himself to what the rightful owner was not using.

'Miss Haynes would let good Julie mango fall on the ground and rot,' he said.

After much persuasion, and reluctant to relinquish the cherished right to punish, Mrs Scobie accepted a compromise: she would hit the strap noisily against the wall, and Little Scobie would holler and beg for mercy as if in desperate pain. Miss Haynes, on hearing such sure sounds of punishment, was satisfied, and Little Scobie, in demonstration of his gratitude, began to save a couple of mangoes for his dear parents. So everybody was happy, although Miss Haynes still felt that she should have the tree cut down. But after all, she was not the rightful owner, whatever the Scobies might have imagined. She was only a tenant.

The house was full of memories and associations for Rufus. Years ago, he had had countless overnight stays there with Twinkle, as Miss Haynes sometimes used to look after him when Auntie Mavis was out of the island on business. On one such occasion, he had sustained a deep gash on the sole of his left foot from an old, rusty can. The distraught Miss Haynes had almost lost her mind with worry. Fortunately, with her knowledge of first aid, she had been able to cleanse and bandage the wound so well that Rufus's foot had not rotted before her eyes as she had feared. Then there was the time when Rufus had been stung in the face by 'Jack Spaniards', the local species of wasps. The swelling had reduced his eyes to two narrow slits, causing the children in the neighbourhood, Little Scobie foremost among them, to laugh at him and call him 'Chinee, Chinee, chinky eye'.

The distressing experience of Twinkle's death would never be erased from Rufus's psyche. Mr Scobie had repeatedly complained to Miss Haynes that the dog, not satisfied with scavenging through his dustbin and scattering the contents, was relieving herself all over his backyard. Rufus himself had heard the string of swear-words and expressive coinages uttered by Mr Scobie whenever he stepped in excrement. He had heard the sinister mutterings by Mr Scobie as he scooped up the refuse, the threats to 'fix that pothound', the ominous hints that Twinkle would pay. He did his level best to keep Twinkle on Miss Haynes's side of the fence – all to no avail. He knew not what form Mr Scobie's vengeance would take, but he was sure that vengeance was coming: maybe Mr Scobie would beat Twinkle with a stick and maim her; maybe he would stone her and take out her remaining eye. It did not enter his mind that Mr Scobie would poison her.

The dastardly deed was done during the long vacation. Twinkle was expecting her first litter and had been howling all night, so at first light, Rufus went to see what was wrong. He immediately started bawling when he saw her lying in her vomit, seemingly unable to move any part of her body, unable even to open her eye. Having rushed outside in response to the alarm, Miss Haynes looked at Twinkle, shook her head and offered the lofty comment:

'This is what you get for living next door to low-class people.'

She did all that she could to save Twinkle. She measured out a quantity of guava leaves, guava bark and cashew bark, and boiled them together. Then she sweetened the mixture, poured some into a feeding bottle and let it cool under running tap water. Twinkle drank readily but listlessly, as Rufus watched for some sign of improvement. She willingly accepted the second dose half an hour later, but by then, she was no longer even moaning, and Miss Haynes was trying to get Rufus to go inside the house. He stayed with Twinkle and watched, and knew when she drew her last breath.

Miss Haynes must have felt she had said enough. She said no more when Rufus asked: 'What happened to her? Did they poison her?'

He might have guessed.

The Rufus that Auntie Mavis took back home on her return to Trinidad was inconsolable and unrecognizably embittered; the belief that there had been foul play remained lodged in his mind.

'How can you be so sure?' she asked.

'I just know,' he replied. 'Mr Scobie poisoned my dog. I don't ever want to see him again. I don't want to stay there again.'

No one but Mr Scobie knew why Little Scobie had been given the name 'Aristophus'. Mrs Scobie had chosen the name 'Michael'. Mr Scobie had agreed. Yet he went and registered the boy under the name 'Aristophus'. When she found out, Mrs Scobie threatened to pour hot oil on her husband, who, in turn, threatened to beat her up if he ever found himself scalded. Fortunately for the survival of the marriage and both parties, the matter was laid to rest there. Through a spontaneous exercise of good sense, everybody avoided the name 'Aristophus', and Aristophus Scobie became known to all, including his parents, as 'Little Scobie'.

Little Scobie was a big man now, enjoying growing fame as a budding calypsonian and known in calypso circles as 'The Mighty Fledgeling'. He would sit on the steps at the front of his parents' house and stare at the barbed-wire fence now protecting the mango-tree yard. And he would compose. Every Carnival season, he would produce two calypsos, which would earn him enough to pay for his Carnival costume. He was unable to hold a job for any length of time, his reputation as a day-dreamer being consolidated with each new assignment. He often said that he was not lacking in ambition, just waiting to discover what his true ambition was. Five years older than Rufus, he had watched with almost big-brotherly pride as Rufus, lankier and lankier by the minute, spurted up to pass him by an inch or so. 'I used to be able to drink soup from a dish on your head. Is I who used to wipe your bottom and change your diapers,' he would say to Rufus, to remind him of his youth and put him in his place. Rufus had doubts about the veracity of such claims, but never bothered to dispute them. He felt that he would have liked to have Little Scobie as a big brother, and he knew that he could get his revenge, at will, by addressing Little Scobie as 'Aristophus'.

'Rufus,' Little Scobie called out, 'you just crossed my mind.' His earnestness didn't conceal the gratuitous lie, but he was genuinely overjoyed to see Rufus. He was beginning to get bored sitting on the steps humming to himself and wondering if he would have enough money to make the final payment on his costume, Carnival being less than a week away. It would be touch and go, because the proceeds from his singing in the calypso tent during the current season had been meagre, to say the least. He had just been thinking that if something didn't happen soon, he would have to go to the café and see if he could locate some action. Inactivity and activity, he found, were most pleasurable in carefully balanced doses.

'Miss Haynes not home, you know,' he informed Rufus.

'Any idea when she coming back?'

'Any minute now,' replied Little Scobie, eager for company and knowing full well that Miss Haynes wouldn't be back for some time.

'How the calypso business going, man?'

Little Scobie heaved a sigh before launching into his well-rehearsed lament:

'Rufus, boy, they will squeeze a little fellow dry, dry, dry. If you know how they wouldn't give a little fellow a chance in this business. All they want is to steal my calypso to make money for themself. All them big-name calypsonian is crooks. The whole lotta them. Only wanting to steal the little fellow calypso, and wouldn't give him a chance to record.'

'But I hear you are singing in a calypso tent this Carnival season,' Rufus said.

Little Scobie sucked his teeth noisily.

'They have me on the bench almost every night. The big boys 'fraid competition. They don't want the public to see me perform on the same stage as them. I tell you, they will suck a little fellow dry, dry, dry.'

'You going back to the tent next season?'

Little Scobie pondered, before replying gloomily:

'Calypso is my life. That is the problem. Some people born to be brain surgeons. I born to sing calypso. If I don't compose calypso, I will die. That is the problem of the artist in this country today.'

Little Scobie was faithful to his theme for over fifteen minutes, while Rufus, a sympathetic mountain of patience, nodded and grunted in compassion, with an occasional question or comment to prompt further elaboration on the same plaint. Eventually, however, Little Scobie, much to his own surprise, was overcome by guilt at having kept Rufus waiting in vain for Miss Haynes. It suddenly occurred to him that Rufus might be pressed for time.

'Don't let me keep you back if you have somewhere to go in a hurry, you know,' he said, full of penitence. 'I realize you are a busy man.'

Little Scobie realized no such thing. He had no idea what Rufus did in life. On seeing the latter walk up to the house next door after so many years, he had deduced that Miss Haynes was the object of the visit. But he had forgotten to ask himself why, in his eagerness for the company of a sympathetic listener. Now the unusual feeling of guilt gave place to the more familiar desire to know. So when Rufus showed no sign of leaving to get on with his busy schedule, Little Scobie ventured to remark:

'Miss Haynes feeling low, low, low these days. She say nobody don't come to see her because she can't do nothing to help nobody, not even herself. She say everybody forget she still alive. She say this world full of ungrateful people. Rufus, boy, ingratitude is one hell of a thing. I can tell you from my own experience.'

It was as if Little Scobie were saying 'Shame on you!', as if it were Rufus's turn to feel guilty.

'Boy, you know how it is' was what he offered to excuse his failure to look Miss Haynes up. He was sure that neither the Scobies nor Miss Haynes imagined it was sheer coincidence that he never stayed with Miss Haynes or visited her house after Twinkle died. The connection was too obvious. Still, he could hardly avoid feeling just a little bit guilty.

In the old days, Auntie Mavis used to take him to see Miss Haynes at least one Sunday a month, after lunch. Rufus used to look forward to the outing. With his shoes shining, socks pulled all the way up to his calves, and hair neatly combed and parted down the middle, he would jump into the car and honk the horn with impatient abandon until Auntie Mavis came running out, threatening to teach him a lesson by denying him the outing the next time. But Rufus knew he was safe. Auntie Mavis would not deny herself the monthly game of '500 rummy' with Miss Haynes, while Rufus went about abetting Little Scobie in provoking the dogs in the neighbourhood.

But that was before Little Scobie had introduced him to the boys on Rigault Lane, before Rufus had begun to assert his passion for sports and games. And when Twinkle died, Auntie Mavis could see the pain Rufus was suffering and understood his reluctance to accompany her.

'In any case,' he argued, 'it's no use taking me to see Miss Haynes. She has nothing to say to me. She is only interested in playing cards with you. Why don't you just drop me off by Rigault Lane?'

Auntie Mavis couldn't fault Rufus's statement on grounds of fact. And after boring him with vague reminders about the selfless deeds Miss Haynes had performed on his behalf, she let him have his sports and games on Rigault Lane.

Miss Haynes took offence, but held her peace. She grumbled as she shuffled the cards. She muttered sullenly as she added up the score. She whined and sighed as she played the winning hand. A couple of months later, she suspended belief when Auntie Mavis sent word that she would be unable to come – because of car trouble. As the months went by without further visits, Miss Haynes remarked to Mrs Scobie that some people apparently sent their cars out of the country for repair. And she started cheating against herself at patience.

In later years, Auntie Mavis would occasionally plead with Rufus to pay Miss Haynes a little visit, so as to let her know he hadn't forsaken her and to convey to her the best regards of the rest of the family. But Auntie Mavis never bothered to find out if Rufus did in fact go, and Rufus, interpreting her failure to ask as a dispensation from the obligation, stayed away from Belmont Circular Road. He therefore had some reason to feel guilty when Little Scobie made his observation on ingratitude.

It was probably that feeling of guilt that caused him – despite his previously firm intention not to give the slightest clue as to the purpose of his unexpected visit – to reveal all to Little Scobie. The latter listened intently, never interrupting once, which was totally out of character for him. His first remark when Rufus was through ('Things like this must not happen') did little to reflect the extent to which he was affected by what he had just heard. Little Scobie had always tended to overemphasize the injustices of the world; for once he felt inadequate to emphasize them enough. He had never had the energy to go into action in order to redress the injustices he thought he saw everywhere; for once he felt the energy thrust into him. Allured then by the urge to redress the injustice done to Rufus, as well as by the prospect of elucidating a mystery, he resolved to reveal all he knew.

There had been no need to swear Miss Haynes to secrecy. She had always prided herself on her ability to keep a secret. She had never breathed to a soul a single word about the circumstances surrounding Rufus's birth. But in a moment of deliberate indiscretion, no doubt prompted by the feeling, after the monthly visits had ceased, that her continuing silence had been taken for granted, she had dropped a few tantalizing clues to a probing Mrs Scobie.

'It look like Rufus and his aunt give you up for good,' Mrs Scobie remarked from the sink where she was washing clothes at the back of her house. A more enticing conversation gambit Miss Haynes did not need, and she began to rail against the short memories of the ungrateful:

'A lot of people behave as if they forget where they come from. They too high and mighty. But pride must come before a fall, I tell you. And when the skeletons come out of the cupboard, they going to be hiding their heads in shame. You mark my words.'

Mrs Scobie had long since mastered that fine art of marking every syllable while scrubbing out every unhappy trace of dirt from the garment before her. Continuing the regular downward-upward motion, she decided to try to narrow the scope of Miss Haynes's all too general observations with the objection:

'But nobody could say the Lintons have skeletons to hide. I could put my head on a block that they are one of the most upright families in this country, if not the most upright.'

Mrs Scobie was in the habit of offering to put her head on a block. She seldom attached to her own words the credence she sought to inspire in the listener, and there was never a butcher around to put her assertions to the test. Miss Haynes, for her part, was no fool; she recognized the bait, but made no effort not to swallow it.

'So why you think Mavis used to pretend to be so nice, bringing Rufus to see me and trying to butter me up?'

Mrs Scobie volunteered no answer.

'If Rufus knew the true situation,' Miss Haynes continued. 'If he found out all the lies that woman has been telling him, he would hold his head and bawl. The shame would stink to high heaven.'

On the question of shame, Miss Haynes would have been hard put to it to deny that she felt somewhat ashamed of herself. She sensed she had gone too far, had been too malicious in her insinuations. Malice didn't come easily to her; the discreet, secretive side took over. While making no effort to retract, to repair any damage she might have done, she would not be drawn any further, she would not swallow any more of the juicy pieces of bait Mrs Scobie kept dangling.

So as she hung the clothes out to dry, Mrs Scobie gave free play to her imagination. She didn't have to be a master detective to understand that the skeleton in the Linton cupboard had to do with Rufus. Her powers of deduction had convinced her that he was born next door on the very day that Grenada was devastated by a hurricane – a conviction she had reached with the benefit of hindsight. Her recollection of the day was graphic. It was towards the end of September 1955. It was her day off from her job as a domestic, so she knew it must have been a Wednesday. The year 1955 had stuck in her mind because Little Scobie was just turning five, and she was planning a birthday party for him – the first he was to have.

In the midst of unending torrential rain and warnings on the radio that a hurricane by the name of Janet was in the area, there were unusual comings and goings next door, and she observed a woman she knew to be a midwife entering Miss Haynes's house. She immediately realized the futility of straining her ears to filter out the extraneous sound of buckets of rain pelting down on the roof to the ear-splitting accompaniment of the rushing wind and pealing thunder.

She remembered that the following day, as news of the disaster in Grenada was coming in, she was puzzled and surprised to hear a baby crying next door. She continued to hear the baby for over a month. She ruled out Miss Haynes as the mother, but despite her clandestine monitoring of the house from behind the curtains of her bedroom window, she failed to witness the departure of mother with baby. Then some eight years later, Little Scobie reported to her that Rufus, who by now was being left next door from time to time, was laying claim to a mango Little Scobie had captured, on the grounds that he, Rufus, had been born in the house closest to the mango-tree. Little Scobie was objecting that Rufus couldn't possibly have been born in the house with the mango-tree, because Miss Haynes had no children. Called in to arbitrate, Mrs Scobie found in favour of Rufus, arguing to herself that by a fluke she now had in her presence someone who could finally shed some light on the eight-year-old mystery.

'Don't tease him, Little Scobie. It is his mango. Don't let his mother come and find him crying.'

'She not my mother. My mother in Venezuela,' said Rufus as he disappeared with the recovered mango. Mrs Scobie reasoned that a little child wouldn't lie about a thing like that. That evening, when Miss Linton came to pick Rufus up, Mrs Scobie distinctly heard him refer to her and address her as 'Auntie'. And there the matter had rested.

But now, after the conversation with Miss Haynes, another thought occurred to her. A little child wouldn't have lied about a thing like that. But suppose he had unwittingly come to believe a lie others had told him? Hadn't Miss Haynes made it clear that Mavis Linton had lied to Rufus about something very important? Yes, that had to be it. They had led the boy to believe that his mother was somewhere else, so that his real mother could masquerade as his aunt, thus safeguarding her reputation and the name of the Linton family. The speed of her intuitive process amazed and impressed Mrs Scobie, and she was quick to report her findings.

'You know, Mavis Linton is that little boy's mother,' she announced proudly to Mr Scobie that evening.

'How you know that?' asked her husband, as Little Scobie pricked up his ears.

'Is Miss Haynes who told me.'

Armed with the memory of that exchange, Little Scobie now resolved to let Rufus have the benefit of the facts.

'Things like this must not happen,' Little Scobie repeated. 'They can't hide from a man where he came from. Anyway, I think I can understand why in a case like this they wanted to hide who the mother is. This is really a case of shame and scandal in the family.'

'What you mean by that?' asked Rufus.

Little Scobie felt his resolve shaking.

'You really don't know what I mean?'

'If you have something to say, say it,' was Rufus's impatient reply.

'What I mean is … This brother and sister business … It might have been a case of rape … '

'What brother and sister business? What rape?'

'So you want me to spell it out for you? Your Uncle Clive and your Auntie Mavis.'

'You must be crazy!' Rufus exclaimed.

'But you know Clive is your father.'

'Yes, but Auntie Mavis is not my mother.'

'That's not what Miss Haynes said.'

'Miss Haynes?' said Rufus in disbelief.

'Yes, man. You know how many years now she told my mother Mavis is your mother?'

As they both fell silent, Rufus cast his mind back to his reaction on reading his birth certificate and to his conversations on the matter with Auntie Mavis. Could he have been too quick to rule out the possibility of incest? Auntie Mavis had said that she did more for him than his own mother. Surely that was irrefutable proof that she was not his mother. Or was it just another attempt to protect the cover-up? After all, she had never said she was not his mother. But he hadn't asked her, had he? There were people who said she was his mother. Miss Haynes had said so. Mrs Scobie had said so. Little Scobie had said so. What was going on here? Who was telling the truth and who was lying? What reason would Miss Haynes have to tell a lie like that? Had she in fact said what Little Scobie alleged?

'So you come to see the Scobies, and you wouldn't even come to see poor ole Miss Haynes?' said the voice from the front steps next door.

'Miss Haynes, you will live long,' replied Rufus, starting out of his socks. 'We were just talking about you.'

'A modern man like you believing in that stupid superstition? According to that, I should live to be at least 150 years old, because people always have things to say about me just before I appear on the scene.'

Having appeased Miss Haynes with the assurance that he had come to Belmont Circular Road specially to see her, and having taken leave of a glum-looking Little Scobie, Rufus made his way into the living-room next door. It took Miss Haynes some time to believe that Mrs Judith Linton had sent Rufus to see her.

'I'm sure your grandmother hasn't lost her memory,' she said bitterly. 'What can I tell you that she doesn't know?'

'I have a right to know what is what,' Rufus pleaded.

'You had a right was to keep yourself quiet and not try to stir up this old business. This thing is going to cause confusion, you mark my words. And I don't want anybody to say is I who start the confusion. Why your grandmother wants me to do the dirty work? She don't find I did enough already?'

'Is it true,' Rufus ventured to ask, 'that Auntie Mavis is really my mother?'

'What?'

'Is Auntie Mavis really my mother?'

'Who told you that, boy?'

'Little Scobie said you told his mother that.'

'Conniving!' she sneered, reaching into her vocabulary for the one word that could describe the lowest form of life.

'Conniving!' she repeated. 'That woman is a conniving, malicious liar!'

Each syllable was articulated with such crisp and deliberate diction that Mrs Scobie would surely have withered had she been present to savour the accolade.

'I never told her that. That is a downright lie. Is a bad thing to have to live next-door to lower-class people. I tell you, is a bad thing.'

Rufus cracked his knuckles, and allowed his anger time to subside. Good-neighbourliness on Belmont Circular Road was not his immediate concern. He had to bring the conversation back to the point.

'If Auntie Mavis is not my mother, then who is?'

'I don't want anybody to say is I who start the confusion,' Miss Haynes repeated. 'You go back to your grandmother and tell her I say that I have no secret to hold and no secret to reveal. This is not my business, boy, and I want no further part of it. Blood thicker than water. Let the high-and-mighty Lintons wash their dirty clothes for themselves. And you could quote me on that before your dear Auntie Mavis, to boot. Yes, give her the same message from me.'

Sally

The suspicion that he was being deliberately sent on a wild-goose chase didn't fail to cross Rufus's mind. All the same, he simply didn't know what to make of the whole business. He was fully convinced that his mother wasn't living across the Gulf of Paria in Venezuela, as he had been led to believe. She was probably someone he saw quite often, someone he would never suspect. But could it be Auntie Mavis? Once again, the spectre of incest intimidated Rufus. He was sure that the motive behind the apparent cover-up had to be shame. But whose shame was it? His conversations with Auntie Mavis, his grandmother, Little Scobie and Miss Haynes had afforded but tiny glimpses of an ever more elusive truth which he continued to circle without approaching. Trapped in that orbit, he was tempted to give up. What good would it serve, he wondered, to try and uncover the shame of the Lintons? What good would it do him to discover his mother's identity?

So though he felt he was too close to the truth to give up now, he decided to suspend the active search, to sit back and wait for something to happen.

Two things did happen before too long. The first had to do with Sally Johnson, a young lady to whom Rufus had been especially attentive for many years. They had known each other since Rufus was 10, and, as Rufus often said to her, they had met because of the Great Underwear Question. Rufus was in the first form at the time. Like many of the boys in his class, he had not yet begun to wear long trousers; unlike many of them, he had not yet begun to wear underpants. It was Auntie Mavis's fault: though she insisted that he always wear a merino vest, she entertained the antiquated notion that boys under a certain age didn't need to wear underpants. Besides, she was thinking how expensive it was to clothe him … already. He was growing at such a rate that it was hard just to keep him in outer garments and shoes, and he was becoming less and less amenable to the idea of wearing cousin Tony's hand-me-downs. Rufus, for his part, was desperate to graduate into long trousers, if only to be spared further teasing about his knees, which, according to his tormentors, looked as if he had avocado stones in them.

The fact that he wore no underpants was noticed by an observant classmate one day when, as it happened, Rufus was sitting in a rather careless position. The observant classmate felt it his duty to bring it to the attention of the community, for which services Rufus – whose blood had been known to boil in reaction to less provocation than that – challenged him to a fight after school, having first warned him to stop spreading the news 'under pain of pain'. The point of honour was settled beneath the spreading branches of a samaan tree, with a circle of bloodthirsty spectators urging on the punches, kicks, clinches and headlocks with a chant of 'Heave! Heave! Heave!' The observant classmate went home with a swollen lip; Rufus went home with both his avocado stones bruised, and with a well-rehearsed lie about a tackle and a fall on the playing-field.

Auntie Mavis wasn't convinced, but not because his story was implausible. The observations that had led people to call him a 'ball whore' were correct, for where you saw a ball being kicked or thrown or bowled or batted, there you would see Rufus. He couldn't bring himself to bypass any ball game in progress, and he often had the cuts and bruises to prove it. Yet with her seemingly supernatural faculty for detecting his lies, Auntie Mavis listened to his story, then told him, as she had told him on previous occasions, that he made a terrible liar. When she extracted the truth, she laughed until she coughed. But by the end of the week, Rufus had five pairs of Jockey shorts, and had been measured for long khaki trousers.

That was the beginning of Rufus's discomfort: the trousers felt too tight, the Jockey shorts too constricting. He was constantly rearranging himself and being accused of fidgeting. He began to ask himself questions about underwear: Who invented it, and why? Matters came to a head in a history class. The boys were taking turns reading aloud from a book about the Arawaks, but Rufus was barely listening. He was too busy studying the illustrations. Of all the drawings – of people, of tools, of huts, of canoes – it was the drawings of the people that held Rufus's attention. Both the men and the women were scantily clad, wearing what looked like loincloths.

The teacher hadn't yet noticed Rufus's raised hand, and Rufus didn't wait to be acknowledged. He blurted out as if in desperation:

'Sir, did the Arawaks wear underwear?'

It seemed to the history teacher as if a virulent epidemic of lunacy had in an instant afflicted his wards. Those who were not shrieking convulsively were banging on their desks or making other loud contributions to the general pandemonium. Even if the teacher had known the answer, he would still have seen the asking of the question as a wilful attempt to be disruptive. He assumed that Rufus was only pretending to be startled at the uproar, and that he had artfully provoked it. When the disturbance was eventually quelled, he pronounced the sentence:

'Linton, you will write for me "The way of the transgressor is exceedingly difficult" three hundred times. And for the

edification of the class you will write a thousand-word essay entitled "Life in the New World before the Coming of Columbus".
We will hear it next Monday.'

Rufus protested in vain: he hadn't meant to create any disrup-
tion; he really wanted an answer to the underwear question;
wasn't the teacher always encouraging them to ask questions if
there was anything they didn't understand? To the accompaniment of mounting commotion and expressions of exaggerated
commiseration, Rufus was sent out of the room.

The public library had two outdated encyclopaedias.
Although a few volumes were missing, Rufus was able to find
ample information on his topic, and easily lifted entire sentences
for his essay. It was when he sought information on underwear –
to satisfy his intellectual curiosity – that he was disappointed. In
the index, he looked for 'Underwear', 'Underclothing' and
'Undergarment', and didn't even find those words. Then he read
the articles under 'Clothing' and 'Apparel' line by line. By the
end, his head was spinning, what with all the descriptions and
pictures of all manner of traditional costumes, uniforms, robes,
dresses, skirts, loincloths and breeches. And still he could find no
mention of underwear.

So he went and asked the librarian if she knew of any books on
underwear. Among those within earshot who started giggling
was Sally Johnson, returning some books at the counter, but she
was sharp enough to notice the tears welling up in his eyes as he
turned to walk out. When she caught up with him outside, she
apologized and introduced herself. They found they had a lot to
say to each other, and the subject of underwear was not
mentioned.

Rufus was well liked by the Johnson family. They saw in him
almost everything they could wish for in a future son-in-law
(even though Sally protested that he was a good five years

73

younger than she): intelligence combined with a serious mind and an ambitious nature. Rufus spent much of his time at their house and was made to feel perfectly at home. Mr Johnson had confided to his wife that Rufus was in a sense a substitute for the son they had given up trying for – given up after having five daughters. Rufus's popularity had extended even to the parents of Mrs Johnson. Her father was often heard to say that Rufus was one of the few members of the younger generation who had any sense of maturity and discipline, discipline being the cardinal virtue Mr Matthews sought to practise and promote. It was, after all, to his innate discipline that he attributed his rapid rise from police corporal to police inspector. Once thus elevated, he had found it inconsistent with the dictates of respectful discipline to be addressed as 'Mr Matthews' by the members of the general public, to whom he became first 'Inspector Matthews' and, in later years, 'Dr Inspector'. He never did get promoted above the rank of inspector, one rumour explaining that he had ruined his chances for good by trying to discipline a senior officer whom he had failed to recognize as such. And as he remained 'Dr Inspector', the members of the general public, with their usual forgetfulness, forgot that his name was Matthews and began calling his wife 'Mrs Inspector'. So when Dr Inspector used to say, out of admiration for Rufus, that 'discipline is the one thing that could make or break a man', he knew exactly what he was talking about.

Several years after first meeting Sally, Rufus concluded he was in love with her. He had finally overtaken her in height and was getting too gangly for his own liking, one day feeling knock-kneed, the next day bow-legged. By this time, not only had Sally become the main subject of his day-time reveries, but she had begun to feature prominently in his night-time erotic dreams as well. He felt increasingly embarrassed by his powerful urge to kiss her, and was having more and more trouble not acting on it.

Believing he needed some tips on handling his romance, he turned to the experience of his friend Rolo. With behind-the-scenes coaching from Rolo, he found a way to declare his love to Sally.

'I just don't know how to tell her,' he confided.

'Will she let you hold her hand?' Rolo asked.

'I think so.'

'Hold her hand and look straight into her eyes,' Rolo advised. 'Don't say a word and don't smile. Sooner or later, she is bound to smile. Ask her what she's smiling at. She'll probably say "Nothing". Then you say "It's no use smiling. All I know is that I love you". And that is all. Don't say another word. Whatever you do, don't ask her if she loves you.'

At the earliest opportunity, Rufus put the technique to the test. But when he attempted to hold Sally's hand, he was immediately sorry that Rolo had not taught him a sure way to overcome coyness. It was not until the fourth attempt that he succeeded in retaining her hand. Then, looking straight into her eyes and following the plan to the letter, he declared himself. The smile vanished from Sally's face; she said nothing and did not look particularly enthralled.

How disheartened he was! How ecstatic he would have been to hear her declare her love for him! But he remained hopeful that she would eventually do so, and they continued seeing each other with the same regularity as before. On Rolo's advice, however, he did not repeat his declaration, did not ask Sally if she loved him in return. Days turned into weeks, weeks into months, months into years, and still the waiting game continued. Not once was the subject broached, even though Rufus did occasionally come close to raising it. Yet at other times, he virtually forgot that he was supposed to be in love, and the goal of discovering whether his love was requited retreated to the furthest recesses of his mind. It was put out of his mind entirely in the aftermath of Dr Inspector's death.

Rufus would never forget the day Dr Inspector died, for it was he who found him dead when he returned from the corner shop with the five cigarettes. It wasn't unusual for Rufus to be sent to buy cigarettes. Yet he always thought it odd that Dr Inspector would never get a whole packet, preferring to have five sticks at a time; it wasn't as if Dr Inspector couldn't afford to buy his cigarettes by the packet or even by the carton, but when anyone told him that he was simply making the shopkeeper rich, or pointed out how much he could save by consolidating his purchases, he would just look at them with indifference and say: 'I know, I know.'

Rufus found him lying on his back with his eyes closed. There was nothing alarming about that either; Dr Inspector enjoyed smoking in bed, and Rufus sometimes had to rouse him from a snooze to give him his change and his five cigarettes. It was only when Dr Inspector failed to stir that Rufus panicked.

Within a fortnight, the will was read. The day after the will was read, Mrs Matthews ordered her daughter to forbid Sally to see Rufus. Sally would not hear of it. She demanded an explanation, got one, but still refused to comply. She told Rufus what had happened:

'Grannie says you and I are too closely related to get married.'

'What do you mean?' asked Rufus in puzzled disbelief.

'The Inspector left you some money in his will. "To my grandson Rufus", the will said.'

'But how could that be?' asked Rufus, still puzzled and disbelieving.

'Well, it appears that the Inspector had an outside child and that you are his outside grandchild. It's like in that Harry Belafonte calypso: "Your daddy ain't your daddy, but your daddy don't know." '

'That Harry Belafonte calypso?' Rufus repeated, again in disbelief, but for a different reason. 'Don't you know that is Lord Melody's calypso? Don't you know what happened with "Rum and Coca-Cola" and so many other calypsos?'

'I don't care whose calypso it is, Rufus. The point is that you are apparently part of a little shame and scandal in the family.'

'As if I didn't know,' Rufus muttered to himself, adding aloud: 'But who, then, is my grandmother, if the Inspector was my grandfather?'

'The woman you've always thought of as your grandmother, Mrs Judith Linton.'

'Was that before she got married to the Reverend?'

'It wasn't,' Sally replied. 'That is what has Grannie so upset. It is something that must have happened while Grannie was married to the Inspector and while your grandmother was married to the Reverend.'

'I find all of this very hard to believe,' Rufus said. 'The Inspector never gave me any hint of this.'

'I find it a bit hard to believe too, but Grannie swears that's the way it was.'

'How can she know? Maybe the Inspector didn't mean that I was literally his grandson, but that I was going to become his grandson by marrying you, that I was going to become his grandson-in-law, to be exact.'

At which Sally shook her head vigorously and said:

'The will lists one of the Lintons as one of his children.'

'Which one? Was it Clive, or was it Mavis?' Rufus asked anxiously. 'Which one?'

'From what my mother told me, Grannie was very tight-lipped about it. But we think it's one of the girls.'

When a queasy feeling came over Rufus that evening, he assumed it was a psychological response to what Sally had said to him. Later in the evening, however, the spasms of pain concentrated in his abdomen eventually thwarted his obstinate attempts to ignore them. Every so often the pain would subside slowly and fool him into thinking that it was going away. But then it would build again to a peak. The fact that he spent the greater part of the night on the toilet seat compounded his misery, but not wanting to disturb Auntie Mavis, he waited till the roosters started their pre-dawn routine. Only then did he go to her for help.

Auntie Mavis was susceptible to colic. She therefore avoided foods that disagreed with her, and was careful to have her meals at regular hours. Whenever she had an attack, she would blame it on gas and seek relief from a special tea. She prepared it from the leaves of a plant known as 'worm grass', boiling them together with dried orange peel and crushed garlic. She knew the therapeutic properties of many plants – which one would ease a belly ache, which one would cool a fever, which one would stop a fit of vomiting. Her faith in herbal concoctions and other traditional medicinal remedies – derisively dismissed by some of her Caribbean friends as 'bush medicine' – hadn't been shaken during her years in England, where she had suffered from the unavailability of such staples as shining bush and soursop leaves. Luckily for her, her mother would regularly ship her a couple of bottles of Tisane de Durbon. Unlike her mother, she had less faith in Angostura bitters than in Tisane. This preparation, containing extracts from plants in concentrated form, had supposedly been invented in the nineteenth century by a French pharmacist. Legend had it that he observed how fit the animals living in the French Alps were, and became convinced that the herbs and plants growing in the mountains preserved and restored their health and could do the same for people. Tisane had an established market in Trinidad. Having already travelled in bulk from France, the precious preparation used to make its way back to Europe in care packages for Auntie Mavis.

When it came to stomach ailments, Auntie Mavis habitually relied on a diagnosis that was overlaid with a simple, not to say simplistic, dualism: the cause was either gas or worms. Just as the battle against worms had been waged from generation to generation, so too the rules of engagement – the combination of ingredients in the home-made medicines, the frequency of preventive treatments, the remedies against infestation – had been taught from generation to generation. Auntie Mavis had good reason to fear, however, that the generation of Pearl, Tony and Rufus wasn't going to carry on the tradition. Indeed, in his resistance to all the concoctions covered by the generic term of 'worm medicine', Rufus was in complete unity and agreement with his cousins. All three swore never to inflict any form of worm medicine on their own children, except as a severe punishment.

At regular intervals during their childhood, usually – but not always – during the school holidays, Auntie Mavis would talk to the children about worms, so as to prepare them for the concoction she was about to prepare: she could tell – from the way Tony had been peevish lately, from the way Pearl had lost her appetite, from the way Rufus felt so tired – that all three had worms; the worms were draining away the energy from their bodies, and their bodies were suffering because the worms were stealing the nourishment from all the good food they ate; they had to get rid of their roundworms and threadworms, their hookworms and whipworms, not to mention their pinworms and the sinister and ruthless 'Creeping Eruption'! Uncharitably, Clive Linton had once accused Mavis of carrying on the Linton tradition of methodically brainwashing and terrorizing young children. She denied the accusation, but did admit that the mere mention of the word 'worms' had a miraculous effect in curing petulance, restoring energy and appetite, and bringing miscreants to heel. She didn't have to spank or threaten to spank; she simply had to say: 'I think you might have worms.'

Having sought to inspire her three charges for the anti-worms crusade, Auntie Mavis would set about producing for them a foul-smelling, foul-looking, foul-tasting, slimy brown liquid. She would keep it hidden, no doubt for its own protection, and every morning for five consecutive days, she would measure out half of a wine glass for each child. On the sixth day, there would be nothing, but on the seventh day, there would be a dose of senna pods, castor oil or aloes. Who devised this method of torture, Rufus used to wonder.

Resignedly, he accepted the prospect that he would periodically be subjected to torture by worm medicine until he left school and Auntie Mavis's house. He was wrong of course; it was only a form of purgatory, and there was to come a day when he would no longer have to endure the bitter cleansing brew. As it had ended for Pearl when she had turned twelve, and for Tony a couple of years later, it was to end for Rufus after his twelfth birthday. No explanation was given by Auntie Mavis, and none was sought by any of the children. They accepted their good fortune with silent grace.

In just six months Rufus would be 20, so he felt relatively safe from mandatory worm medicine. He wasn't really surprised at Auntie Mavis's suggestion that gas or worms were to be blamed for his present condition, yet he found himself saying to her in a tone of amazement:

'How can any worms still be living in my body? With all the worm medicine and bush medicine you terrorized me into swallowing, all the worms should have been killed and all their larvae destroyed.'

Then, despite his discomfort, he just laughed when she offered to provide him treatment in the form of a course of molasses, charcoal powder and aloes.

'Laugh as much as you like,' she said. 'It will do you more good than penicillin.'

They engaged in a few minutes of banter; but amid it all Rufus was thinking that truth was indeed stranger than fiction. The more he pondered upon the allegation that Sally and himself were close blood relations, the more far-fetched he found it. What were the odds against such a coincidence? Inveterate wagerer though he was, he wasn't prepared to lay any.

It was to be expected, however, that a few tentative conclusions would begin to form in Rufus's mind: the Linton child fathered by the Inspector was probably Mavis; that would make her Clive's half-sister; he, Rufus, was therefore the child of Mavis and her half-brother; incest had taken place, but in a degree that made it slightly less intolerable to Rufus.

Carmen

The Inspector's death, then, was one of the two events that prompted Rufus to resume the active search for the truth about his birth. The second event occurred in the aftermath of a surprise visit by Mrs Judith Linton. Rufus came home one evening to find her and Auntie Mavis looking sombrely at each other. After the customary courtesies, he thought it politic to go for a walk, being used to Mrs Linton's unexpected visits. A few days later, Clive Linton took his mother to spend a weekend at his home. Again, there was nothing unusual about that. But Rufus could tell when something was up. Although he overheard no conversations, interrupted no whispered exchanges, he could sense that he was the subject of the many discussions that were undoubtedly taking place within the Linton clan. He was totally unprepared, however, for Clive Linton's statement when he brought his mother back on the Sunday. To say the least, he was unprepared for any utterance by Clive on matters not related to rum or cricket, those being the absorbing passions that had turned Clive into a rum-drinking repository of facts and figures. It was true that, as a rule, Clive Linton didn't like to be asked questions. But questions about cricket were actively encouraged, especially when the spirits began to work on him. He at times became tiresome with his constant challenges to his audience to test his cricketing knowledge. He could name all the members of the first West Indies team to tour England. He would be up in the middle of the night sipping his rum and listening to commentaries on matches taking place in Australia, disturbing his sleeping wife as he talked back to the commentators to correct their errors of fact. He boasted that he had never missed a single day's play of any test match at the Queen's Park Oval since he had reached 'the age of cricketing reason', as he called it.

'No good, self-respecting batsman should ever get clean bowled,' was a favourite dictum of his. 'In cricket, a batsman has a proper bat, not a little stick like in baseball. And he has big, hard pads. And he should be looking at the ball. I can understand him trying to hit the ball over the top and getting caught on the boundary. That I can understand. I can understand him padding up and being given out l.b.w. Or going for a cover drive, getting an edge and being caught behind. Or getting a bad bounce and playing on. But to let the ball miss the bat, miss the pads, miss his whole body and hit the stumps – I can never understand that. No self-respecting batsman should ever let that happen.'

Though Clive loved to entertain his audience by doing the distinctive Garfield Sobers walk to the crease, he was never seen holding a bat – not by Rufus at any rate. Yet he obviously lived for cricket. Because of the conviction and authority with which he spoke, it seldom occurred to any listener that anything he said might be apocryphal. Rufus had no way of verifying Clive's statement that Learie Constantine used to tap the ground with his bat in order to predict exactly how the wicket would play, but it sounded true enough.

A name that stuck in Rufus's mind was 'Leslie Hylton', not because of his cricketing exploits – according to Clive, Hylton had been a mediocre fast bowler – but because of the year 1955. The year Rufus was born was the year Hylton was hanged for the murder of his wife. Over and over again, Clive would talk about the time Hylton had toured England, with Constantine, the Stollmeyers and Headley, in 1939.

'Hitler made them run back to the West Indies,' Clive would say melodramatically. 'They had to cancel some minor matches in order to catch the boat. And a good thing too! Ten days after the last test, Germany invaded Poland! That was the last team to tour England before World War II. It was the sixth West Indies team to tour England. The next time was in 1950, when Ramadhin and Valentine bamboozled the English batsmen.'

One of Clive's abiding regrets was that Sobers had chosen Sabina Park in Jamaica, and not the Queen's Park Oval in Trinidad, to score 365 not out against Pakistan in 1958. He had, however, been listening enraptured to the radio commentary, and he had later read all the reports he could lay his hands on. Thus he went beyond his metamorphosis into an eyewitness till he reached the point where he could act out with plausible fidelity his account of Sobers's array of strokes during that famous innings.

'Gary was only 21 years old. Can you believe that?' he would say, twisting his face in mild incredulity, or at the taste of the Angostura bitters in the rum he was sipping. The more animated he got, the more hirsute he appeared to Rufus. His eyebrows merged into one continuous bushy fringe, the hair around the mole on his left ear-lobe got thicker, the hair peeping out of his nostrils grew longer.

'It was his first century in a test match,' Clive would continue, 'and he could have made more than 365. He could have scored over 500. Those Pakistanis were never going to get him out. And you know something. That man Sobers so merciless, so wicked, in the very next test, the man scored a century in each innings!'

The hands Rufus had never seen holding a cricket bat he had always seen touching people. He had seen the hairy hands talking. He knew that when Clive was trying to make a point, it was wise to step back in order to avoid the poke of the index finger that he used for emphasis. In addition, Clive wanted to embrace and kiss every woman he met. He didn't understand the concept of keeping his hands to himself, oblivious to the signs that not everyone appreciated the misplaced familiarity of his hugs or his way of resting his arms on women's shoulders. At social occasions, he merited first prize for liveliness, gregariousness and jollity, and he got all the women to dance. When he was busy doing his fancy dance steps and trying to keep his hairy stomach from hanging out of his shirt, the wags would joke that his spindly legs were going to break and that his belly looked bigger than usual, much too big for the rest of his body.

Clive liked to boast of his 'physical inability to get drunk'. No one could truthfully say he was the rolling-under-the-table type. He seemed perfectly capable of walking in a straight line and manoeuvring his car safely, even after downing quantities of rum which, if one was to believe his mother, accounted for the progressive bloating of his stomach and the invisible, but no less certain, poisoning of his liver. Yet, those who claimed to know him well also claimed to be able to tell when he had reached his non-drunken state of drunkenness – by his tendency to become melancholic, hypersensitive and tearful at the slightest pretext, and repeat another of his favourite dicta: 'You can kick me, cuff me, butt me, do me anything you want, but just don't criticize me. That's the only thing I can't take.' He had learned to ignore Mavis's criticism of his dressing habits. She no longer objected so forcefully when he kept his pyjama suit on all Saturday as he relaxed in and around his house. What thoroughly disgusted her was his consummation of the marriage between home clothes and going-out clothes by leaving his house while wearing pyjama trousers as underpants.

On the Sunday afternoon when Mrs Linton was escorted into the living-room by Clive, his pyjamas were trying to sneak past the hem of his trousers, and anyone could tell that he had been crying. Rufus was sitting in a rocking-chair, trying to keep his thoughts on the book in front of him. Auntie Mavis was in her room digesting her Sunday lunch. Clive seized on the fact that she wasn't present to welcome him, affecting to take offence at the slight. He was a man who rarely shouted. But he had the deep, resonant kind of voice that could fill up most rooms. It easily filled up Mavis's room, as he and his mother walked into it:

'But Mavis, where's the food you left for your beloved brother? I was only hearing spoon on plate, spoon on plate when I was parking the car. Like you were eating in a hurry. Like you were eating up all the food to make sure your beloved brother didn't get any. And instead of being out there to greet me, you lying down on your bed!'

'Why don't you stay home and batter your wife instead of coming here to bother me?' Mavis retorted with a smile.

With Mrs Linton contributing some well-aimed barbs, the teasing and joking continued for a few minutes, falling into a pattern which Rufus recognized so well that he stopped listening. He was brought back to a state of attentiveness by the raised voice of his grandmother:

'I will not allow the good name of my family to be destroyed by scandal.'

The ensuing silence was broken by Clive, who said in a firm, insistent tone:

'I have no reason to carry on with this pretence. And I can't continue for the sake of someone who hates me.'

'She doesn't hate you,' Mrs Linton pleaded.

'Yes, she does. She has said as much.'

With that, he strode out into the living-room and, looking like a man anxious to unburden himself before he lost his nerve, blurted out to Rufus, without poking him:

'Boy, you might as well know now. I am not your father.'

Clive didn't expect Rufus to burst out laughing. Rufus surprised himself as well, and in mentally reviewing the episode, he would later reason that he had laughed out of relief, out of a sense of agreeable disappointment. There was, after all, no cause for merriment. The grim fact was that in addition to being of mother unknown – or uncertain – he had suddenly been rendered fatherless. Not that Clive had ever been a father to him, but at least he was a visible presence whom Rufus had accepted without question as his father. He had been wrong to take that for granted. He had been wrong about so many things. He wasn't even born in a hospital.

Yet laugh Rufus did, causing Clive, Mavis and Mrs Linton great discomfiture. The two women had been unprepared for Clive's confession, and even more unprepared for the fit of laughter. When he regained his composure, the first thing Rufus did was to walk over to the glass cabinet where Mavis kept the assorted bottles of liquor which she would offer to visitors with a quaint 'Would you indulge yourself in any strong?' She had never extended such an offer to Rufus, perhaps out of fear that he might develop a taste for liquor and follow in the footsteps of Clive. And, perhaps in order to allay her fears, Rufus had never, in her presence, manifested any great interest in alcoholic beverages, although among his peers he was admired as one who could hold his liquor. Stealing a line from Clive, he had impressed them with the boast that he was physically incapable of getting drunk. As far as Mrs Linton and Mavis were concerned, however, Rufus, at 19, was still at the tender age when even minute amounts of alcohol could cause irreversible brain damage. Worse still, in their eyes, his action in removing a bottle of rum from the cabinet and pouring himself a drink denoted a measure of disrespect that was totally out of order.

'It is not because you wear long pants,' Mrs Linton began, 'that you are a man in this house. It is not because your aunt keeps alcohol in her house that this place is a common rum-shop.'

Rufus smiled and took his first sip. He wasn't swift enough to defend himself as his grandmother snatched the glass from his hand and poured the contents over his head, saying:

'You think you are a big man, big enough to drink rum in my face and show me rudeness. Well not before I baptize you in rum.'

What happened next was to astound those who heard about the incident later. Rufus grabbed as many bottles and glasses from the cabinet as he could and dashed them against the nearest wall. Mavis joined Clive in restraining him, but not before three bottles and a couple of glasses had been smashed. And then Rufus started kicking, biting, flailing about as if he had lost his mind, and screaming some of the foulest combinations of vulgarities his grandmother could remember ever hearing. It was not a Rufus that she, Mavis or Clive recognized. Eventually, Clive managed to overpower Rufus, twisted his arm behind his back, threw him down and kept him pinned to the floor until he started to return to normal.

That, however, proved to be the Sunday of revelation. After Mavis, Clive and Mrs Linton had cleared up the mess and done their best to get the rum-shop smell out of the living-room, they approached Rufus, who was glowering at the space in front of him, and began to explain. In the first place, as Rufus had already discovered, 'Rufus' was not his real name. He had been registered at the Red House as 'Prince Linton'. How, then, had he come to be called Rufus? That had been the bright idea of no one else but Mrs Judith Linton. Her chief concern at the time of Prince's birth had been to avoid the scandal that the news of

14-year-old Carmen having a baby would surely have provoked. Very few people outside the immediate family knew that Prince existed, and those who knew were urged to keep the information to themselves. Only a few weeks after Prince was born, Mavis's sister Linda, then living in Mayaro, Trinidad, gave birth to a boy, whom she named Rufus. That birth was the one Mrs Linton chose to announce to all who came within earshot. Having thus established the existence of a baby boy named Rufus, she started referring to Prince by the name 'Rufus', and invited the rest of the family to do likewise. When the six-week-old Prince was taken from Miss Haynes's house on Belmont Circular Road to live with Mavis, he went with a new name. The curious were told that Linda, who already had five children, had asked Mavis to help her out with the sixth.

Mavis had been presented with a *fait accompli*. True, she had agreed, in advance, to take care of Prince; but she had objected to the change of appellation – that is, when she had been informed of it, belatedly. At the time she was already looking after two children fathered out of wedlock by two of her brothers. That was common knowledge. With a broad-mindedness no doubt fostered during her university days in England, she had argued that there was no need to hide the fact that Prince, too, had been born out of wedlock. Mrs Linton, firmly committed to the double standard, remained adamant:

'Nobody is going to drag my daughter's name through the mud.'

'But who,' Mavis had protested, 'dragged Cecil's name through the mud when I started taking care of his daughter Pearl? And who dragged Graham's name through the mud when I started taking care of his son Tony?'

'That is a different matter,' Mrs Linton had maintained. 'With men it is a different matter.'

'Well, why not say that one of them is Prince's father?' Mavis had asked.

For a split second, Mrs Linton had had to admit to herself that she hadn't thought of that particular angle of deception. But before she had had time to kick herself, she had seen and voiced an objection:

'Cecil and Graham are both married now. That would only cause confusion and comess with their wives.'

'Well, what about Clive then?' Mavis had asked, causing her mother to remember an objection she had seen, but failed to voice, a few seconds earlier: having put it abroad that Prince, now Rufus, was the son of her daughter Linda, she couldn't, without risk of great scandal, name her own son as the boy's father. But she had kicked herself this time. She ought to have thought of that ploy in the first place. It would have been so simple. Now she couldn't go back. She couldn't or wouldn't turn the Rufus back into a Prince. That name-changing stratagem of hers was one she had considered at such length that she couldn't bring herself to imagine it was advisable to abandon it. At the same time, she saw merit in the suggestion to have Clive identifiable as the boy's father, despite the objection she remembered. And, she told herself, she, with her ability to think quickly, would always be able to find explanations to confuse the over-curious and put them on the wrong scent. After all, there did exist a Rufus who was the son of her daughter Linda. Well, then, the other Rufus was Clive's son. She had two grandsons bearing the name Rufus. Who had ever said that the Rufus living with Mavis was Linda's son? There must have been some misunderstanding.

Pre-armed with explanations, Mrs Linton and Mavis had contacted Clive, then working with an oil company in southern Trinidad. With deep misgivings, he had agreed to go along with the pretence. Even after his marriage to Sheila, he had kept his part of the bargain, doing nothing to correct the false image she had of him as one who had got some poor girl into trouble. Many a time he had been sorely tempted to spill the beans, especially after he had a falling-out with Rufus's mother. They were no longer on speaking terms.

The revelation of his mother's identity had little, if any, immediate visible effect on Rufus. He appeared to have reached a state of serenity where nothing further could hurt, move or affect him in any way. Carmen, the youngest of the Lintons, was not a person with whom he felt the slightest affinity. She displayed none of the warmth towards Rufus and the other children that came so naturally to Mavis. Carmen's presentation of gifts (always expensive), at Christmas, birthdays and other occasions meriting such gestures, seemed to be prompted by little more than a sense of obligation. Rufus could discern nothing joyous in those acts of giving. On Christmas Eve she would arrive with a wretched look on her face, engage Mavis in the requisite amount of small talk, leave a pile of presents under the Christmas tree, then depart hurriedly for her home on the hill.

Rufus associated one extremely unpleasant memory with that house in Cascade. He must have been about 10 years old at the time. One Saturday morning, Carmen came to Mavis and asked to 'borrow' Rufus for the weekend. She needed a little help in sprucing up the place for some house-guests she was expecting. Rufus didn't want to go. He wasn't a lazy boy; he willingly did his allotment of chores – and sometimes even more, when he felt like it. What he resented was being expected to help out somebody he didn't particularly care for. But nobody asked him if he wanted to go. To the adults around him, he hadn't yet reached the age when his preferences in such matters might become worthy of notice. It was assumed that unless Mavis voiced any objections, he would be 'borrowed'. And he was.

Another reason Rufus never looked forward to being borrowed by Carmen was that she was a compulsive spanker who would use any nearby object or even her bare hands on a real or perceived culprit, without regard for where the blows landed. Her vitriolic admonitions always provided an accompaniment to the blows, whose function seemed to be to illustrate, emphasize and reinforce the points she was making. The incident of the wedding-day spanking, or the 'grape-licks', as it came to be called, had by now become part of the family folklore. Auntie Mavis had been helping with the arrangements for a wedding, and had bought a carton of grapes for the occasion. Her mistake had been to store them in the pantry. Unlike the mangoes, bananas and other local fruits, grapes and apples weren't normally seen or eaten outside the Christmas season by Tony, Pearl, Rufus and the other children. The rare treat in the pantry proved irresistible, and when the day of the wedding came, only a handful of grapes remained. It so happened that Auntie Mavis was being accompanied to the wedding by Carmen and her husband, and as they arrived to pick her up, she went to fetch the grapes.

Auntie Mavis promised to get to the bottom of the mystery when she returned from the wedding, but Carmen – who was in no way involved in the arrangements for the wedding and hadn't even known about the grapes beforehand – would have none of it; she insisted on getting to the bottom of the mystery 'this minute', although they were already late for the wedding. She removed the belt from the waist of her son Patrick, whom she was going to leave with his cousins while she attended the wedding, and summoned the children. In addition to Tony, Pearl and Rufus, two children from next door were in the house at the time; they had had no hand in the disappearance of the grapes. Carmen lined up all the children regardless, and bellowed at them, demanding to know who had been at the grapes.

No sooner had Pearl opened her mouth, maybe to explain, maybe to own up, than Carmen let loose with belt and tongue.

'Don't tell me no lies!' she bawled, as Pearl screamed and tried to shelter her face from the flailing belt. The other children, too intimidated to run, instinctively dropped to the floor in a self-protective crouch. Carmen swung the belt wildly and blindly, with all the force she could muster, the impact of the lashes punctuating her tirade about lies, thieves and grapes. The weals on the children's skin were visible for weeks afterwards. As a result of those on the neck of one of the neighbour's children, all relations between the two houses remained severed for years.

Having good reason to be apprehensive that the children might harbour ideas of retribution, Carmen, as a precaution, decided to take Patrick to the wedding with her, even though he was in his home clothes. Panting and looking more fearsome than ever, she yelled at the cowering, crying children that she would never forgive them for stealing the grapes she had bought with her own money and for making her late for the wedding. Rufus remembered that parting bellow as the unkindest cut of all, far more hurtful than the flailing belt.

Polishing the floors was one of the tasks assigned to Rufus when he was borrowed that Saturday morning. Floor-polishing was a chore which he had turned into a fine art. He had come to love the smell of the wax polish as he applied it with a master touch to the parallel floor-boards. He enjoyed the total control he had over the space entrusted to him. All others were forbidden to enter, until he gave the all-clear. He would pretend to be dissatisfied with the finish, while others marvelled at the shine.

The floors in Carmen's house that Rufus was required to polish did not themselves pose a formidable task. It was Patrick, five years Rufus's junior, who made the job difficult. The little boy kept running off with the tin of polish, showing open contempt for Rufus's threat to 'cuff him down'. In the end Rufus, controlling himself, rubbed some polish on the face of the youngster, who went off crying in search of motherly justice. Carmen was furious, and threatened to spank Rufus. She accused him of being a big bully who would gratuitously torment a little baby. Thus encouraged, the little baby became even more of a pest. When he deliberately poured milk on a part of the floor to which the polish had already been applied, Rufus drew on greater reserves of self-control and didn't knock the nuisance down.

Having polished and shone the floors, Rufus was sent to the grocery to buy milk – to replace what the little baby had used on the polish. Having returned, he was put to wash dishes. Having washed the dishes, he was told to grate a coconut. This, for Rufus, was the last straw. He had been tried and tested beyond measure. Coconut-grating was a job he was always most reluctant to perform, no doubt because he so often managed to grate the skin off his knuckles.

At first, Carmen didn't even notice that Rufus was crying. He was standing silently at the kitchen-table, with his back towards her. He didn't sniff; he didn't draw breath; he didn't wipe the tears away. But the tears slowed him down, and, with a few white chunks still waiting to be grated, he stopped altogether.

'What's happening, boy? You've gone on strike already?' Carmen asked as she walked over to see what remained to be done. Seeing the tears pouring out of his eyes, she followed with:

'But what's the matter with you, boy? You letting your salty tears drop into my coconut. Just like that you start crying like a baby? You want something to cry for? Well, I will give you something to cry for.'

And with that, before Rufus could duck out of the way, she landed him one across his face. Rufus was quick to recover. He darted, overturning the bowl, grater and coconut in the process. And as he darted, he started to bawl. He ran down the back stairs and jumped over the low fence separating Carmen's yard from the vacant adjoining lot, all covered with bush. Still bawling, he laid himself down in the bush and continued to bawl. Rufus bawled and bawled and bawled. Eventually, he fell asleep in the bush.

He must have been asleep for a few hours, for it was already getting dark when Carmen's husband, Dennis, came to retrieve him.

'Time to go home now, Rufus,' he said gently. Inside the house, the baby-pest was not so kind. He was laughing at Rufus, pointing his finger and saying 'cry-cry-baby, wollo, wollo dumpling, put your finger in your eye and tell your mother something'. But his father chased him away. Carmen was not in sight. It was her husband who drove Rufus back home. They exchanged not a word during the drive, but as Rufus was getting out of the car, Dennis said to him:

'Don't mind that, Rufus. These are things that are sent to try us. You must take it like a man.'

Rufus was deeply touched by those words.

That experience in Cascade returned to Rufus's mind with a renewed immediacy as Mrs Judith Linton disclosed the secret she had helped her daughter Carmen to preserve for so many years. One question which at once occurred to Rufus was whether Carmen's husband was in on the secret. Had Dennis, Rufus wondered, known, before he got married to Carmen, that

Rufus was her son? And if he had known at that time, how had he reacted? Or had he been informed subsequently? Or was he still in the dark?

Concentrating on such questions, Rufus had little time to ponder what his next step should be, now that he had secured the knowledge he had so desperately sought.

On Wednesday evening he telephoned Carmen – finally getting a connection on about the eighth attempt. He frowned when he heard Patrick's voice on the other end, and almost hung up. But he decided against it.

'Hello, may I speak to Auntie Carmen please?'

'Who's speaking?' Patrick demanded to know.

The question never failed to infuriate Rufus. It was doubly infuriating when it was Patrick who asked it.

'This is Rufus, and I would like to speak to Auntie Carmen if you don't mind.'

'Hold on,' Patrick said roughly. On his return, he informed Rufus:

'My mother can't come to the phone right now. She will call you back.'

She never did.

The next day was the 13th of the month. Rufus was not embarrassed to admit that he was superstitious and was uncomfortable with the number thirteen. Nothing could have impelled him to try to contact Carmen on Friday the 13th. But the next day was a Thursday, and 24 hours made a slight difference. At the College, as he went through the motions of discussing past participles, Hiawatha and a poem about a sycamore tree, all he could do was weigh the pros and cons of initiating a conversation with Carmen on Thursday the 13th. With lingering misgivings, but at least with the satisfaction that he was acting only after due deliberation, he decided to call when he got home.

This time it was her husband Dennis who answered the phone and came back with the message that Carmen would return Rufus's call. But he phrased it differently:

'She said to tell you that she can't come to the phone and that she will call you back.'

What the son had asserted as fact, the husband had reported non-committally. Rufus felt courageous enough to ask:

'Doesn't she want to speak to me, or what?'

'That's a question she will have to answer herself, Rufus. But my own feeling is that she doesn't want to have anything to do with you.'

'Do you know why? What I mean is, do you know what is really behind all this?' Rufus asked.

'I'm not a fool, Rufus. And I'm not blind.'

Before he could say anything further, Carmen, who had apparently been listening in and had grabbed the receiver, shouted to Rufus:

'There is nothing for us to talk about, and I wish you would stop pestering me!'

With that, she hung up.

On Friday the 14th, Rufus did not go to work. He made no attempt to send word that his students would have to learn about 'under the sycamore tree' without him.

He had feared that his skull was fractured, one afternoon, half a dozen years back, when his head had collided with that of another player during a football match. Now the mallet pounding on his brain made his head feel worse than that. He had lost all energy, all strength, all enthusiasm when his beloved dog Twinkle had died, but he had found solace in his books. Now the desire to read had deserted him altogether. If it hadn't, he might have turned to a poem he had read recently with one of his classes – about spring – and persuaded himself that this was the season of hope and renewal. Wasn't it, after all, the middle of March? He might have told himself, as he had told the class, that all of nature was flushed with the excitement of rebirth, signified by the blooming daffodils.

The bored, blank stares from the students had been their way of telling him he was on his own: they couldn't transport themselves with him to a distant land where there was more to a year than a rainy season and a dry season. As far as they knew, there was no spring in the air. Yesterday was hot, today was hot, and tomorrow would be hot.

When the Pollards and the Garcias came calling on Auntie Mavis that Friday evening, Rufus breached the etiquette of the house and departed from the routine that the three children were supposed to follow for as long as they lived under that roof. After coming out to greet the guests and exchange a few pleasantries, they were expected to say goodnight, ask to be excused and retire. But never once that evening did Rufus emerge, as trained, to acknowledge the presence of the visitors and pass the time of day with them. Partly, it was because he was trying to take a shower when they arrived. He was standing beneath the shower-head, wondering whether to wait for another trickle or to towel the lather off his body, and thinking about Zala's comments. 'Turn on the pipe, anytime, night or day,' Zala had said, 'and you get running water in England. But you think the people appreciate it? No. They will sit once a week in a tub of dirty water. In Trinidad, now, they will haul water from the river, carry buckets of water on their head, wash their whole body at a standpipe by the roadside, collect rain water – just to bathe and smell nice. I tell you, Trinidad is a paradise.' Having no illusions about being guaranteed an uninterrupted flow of tap water in paradise, Rufus kept praying for a trickle. Still, he blessed the silence of the shower for permitting him to hear the conversation in the living-room, thereby offering him a welcome respite from thinking about Carmen.

'They say it's a religious march,' Mrs Garcia commented.

'Yes, but what they didn't say is that the religion is communism,' Auntie Mavis pointed out.

'They want to turn this place into a Cuba,' Mr Pollard warned. And Mr Garcia snorted:

'They say they want to march for bread, justice and peace. You ever hear more? We have all of that in Trinidad. We have plenty bread and too much justice. And the peace we have, they want to break it.'

'The police should lock them up!' Mrs Pollard chimed in. 'We might have bread, but we have to line up for hours to get gas for the car. So we can't get gas for the car, we can't get gas to cook, we can't even get sugar to sweeten tea. This country in real trouble.'

More often than not, the discussions Rufus overheard in Auntie Mavis's house involved much talking at cross-purposes and much staunch defending of opposing views, without real passion. That evening, he thought he detected genuine agitation in the voices that wafted into the cubicle, and unusual unanimity too. He towelled off the lather, went to his room and lay down, still listening to the discussion as it grew less animated and more humdrum. He was eventually overcome by its soporific effect, but as the guests were getting ready to leave, he woke up and couldn't go back to sleep – his second straight night of insomnia.

Over the weekend, he tried with all his might not to keep dwelling on Carmen's fleeting words to him, not to keep playing back every second of the telephone episode. Whenever the house fell silent, he failed in that attempt, as in the attempt to rid himself of his thumping headache and stave off the depression that was to overpower him. He did not lose his appetite, though.

Rather he began to eat as if preparing his body for an impending famine. Seeing that he started taking his food to his room, Auntie Mavis understood that for the time being he didn't wish to have meals with her, and she simply left his double portions in the oven. He continued, as in the past, to wash and put away whatever dishes and cutlery he used.

On Monday he went back to work. Never had he been testier. He handed out more than a fair share of detentions. Left and right, he handed them out, for peccadillos he would have ignored a week earlier. By Wednesday everybody, teachers included, knew it was best to stay out of his way. Nobody even asked him his opinion about the events in San Fernando.

It seemed that Rufus was the only person in the country not preoccupied with the events in San Fernando. The nation-wide unrest had been the talk of Auntie Mavis's kitchen on Saturday, with sundry newsmongers – neighbours, friends, relatives – drifting in to massage the latest titbits from the grapevine. The march that her guests had been talking about on Friday evening had been scheduled for the Tuesday. It had been aborted. The 8,000 or so people who had gathered in San Fernando with the intention of holding a procession all the way to Port-of-Spain had been stopped in San Fernando and ordered to disperse. Tear gas had been used against them, and many claimed they had been beaten by the police. On Tuesday evening there had been a blackout lasting about three hours, and the rumour being noised abroad was that electricity workers were showing solidarity with the marchers.

When Rufus got home on Wednesday evening, Auntie Mavis was being subjected to complaints by her brother Clive about the actions of the police in halting the procession in San Fernando:

'You should see how the police was beating them. You would think this was South Africa. They chased the marchers into a Presbyterian Church. That is sacrilege!'

'Were you there?'

Clive remained indignant: 'Look, even the Catholic Archbishop had to speak out against police brutality.'

Rufus was nonplussed by the irreverence of Auntie Mavis's response, especially as she was such a church mouse. This daughter of the Reverend Andrew Linton, an Anglican minister who had once been a Catholic, had made the return journey from Protestantism while at university. Rufus was used to her crusade to restore staunch Catholicism to her part of the Linton clan. He was more used to that than to what she was doing now: hissing and sucking her teeth, making a long 'Steups'. Despite the infrequency with which he heard her producing that sound, he heard it often enough to appreciate what a full register her steups had. Depending on her pattern of stress, the length and pitch of the hiss, and the context in which it was created, one minute it could be playful and good-humoured, whereas the next minute it could convey gradations of impatience, irritation, disparagement, contempt and anger. It was so easy for her to steups that occasionally she didn't even realize she was doing it. This inborn facility of hers – like the effortlessness with which Miriam Makeba could make click sounds while singing – highlighted the paradox of the steups. A routine, wordless expletive, defying phonetic transcription, it was, for Auntie Mavis, so simple, so spontaneous a sound that it might have been expected to come naturally to all of humanity. Yet unlike a shriek, a snort or a grunt, it didn't seem to be a human sound of universal usage. One of Rufus's colleagues on the staff of the College – a mathematics teacher doing Voluntary Service Overseas – was game for the challenge of reproducing the steups, but however much he pursed his lips, screwed up his mouth, and twisted and sucked his tongue, all he ever managed to produce was saliva. It was enough to give Rufus a superiority complex, for though his steups lacked the versatility of Auntie Mavis's, he could certainly hold his own.

At the mention of the Archbishop, then, Auntie Mavis let out a steups. She wrinkled her nose as if it had been offended, commanded her crop of grey to rise, and adopted a tone she would have used with one of her charges a few years earlier, leaving them feeling utterly squashed.

'The Archbishop should keep his tail quiet,' she admonished. 'You would have never seen Count Finbar Ryan say that or get mixed up in that.'

'And what about all the children who were all geared up to take the 11-plus? And now Cabinet postponed the exam! Can you imagine that? After all the cramming, all the money on private lessons and all the worrying. They have the poor children in even more suspense.'

Auntie Mavis grimly and mechanically adopted a defensive position when she sensed an impending attack on the leader she idolized:

'Well, you can't blame Dr Williams for that.'

Rufus could appreciate how difficult it was for 'the poor children in even more suspense'. He, too, had been distracted by an atmosphere of labour unrest at the time he was preparing to write the common entrance examinations. It seemed ages ago. And San Fernando, though less than 30 miles away, might easily have been on the other side of the globe. The postponement of the 11-plus, the power cuts and the resulting postponement of all sorts of functions, the marches and demonstrations, the strikes and threatened strikes, the allegations of police brutality, the demands of the oilworkers and canefarmers – all of that kept fading from his mind over and over and over again.

More than anything else, he wanted to talk to Carmen. He didn't expect anything from her. What could she give him now, out of all that she hadn't given him over the past twenty years? Love?

As a child, he hadn't felt totally unloved. Auntie Mavis had given him love, maybe even a bit more than she had given Pearl and Tony, the two cousins with whom he had grown up. No doubt they had resented him for it. But it wasn't his fault. Few things made Auntie Mavis happier than a child's good school performance. Pearl and Tony had been poor students. Tony was usually at the bottom of his class. At least once he was placed last. He wasn't good at sports either. Pearl hadn't done so badly. On her report card, the teachers often wrote that she was well-behaved and had personality. 'Should try harder', some would say, encouragingly. It was Rufus's report card that always made Auntie Mavis proud. He was usually placed in the second five. On one happy occasion, when two of the top performers in the class had been absent for the end-of-term exam, because of chicken-pox, he was placed third.

Auntie Mavis believed that Rufus should be rewarded for doing well at school, and many a time she gave him a little extra something, more spending money, a ride in the car while Pearl and Tony stayed at home, a more expensive Christmas or birthday present. Like Pearl and Tony, Rufus noticed the difference and knew he was the favourite. He understood why they left Auntie Mavis's home to make it on their own as soon as they were old enough. Pearl went to Port-of-Spain to study nursing, and lived in a nurses' residence. She remained on cordial terms with Auntie Mavis, and occasionally came to visit. Tony had become a total stranger. He drove a taxi on the Port-of-Spain–Diego Martin route. Rufus sometimes saw him picking up and discharging passengers in the Independence Square area, but Tony often seemed not to notice Rufus. Auntie Mavis once complained to Rufus that Tony had failed to stop when she had attempted to flag him down. Rufus could understand why.

On one occasion that was etched eternally on Rufus's memory, Tony had allowed him to enter the taxi, without acknowledging him in the slightest and without interrupting his monologue:

'The other day, one of them PNM politicians say that Trinidad is a sleeping giant. Trinidad ain't have no right to be a sleeping giant. We don't want that. You could kill a sleeping giant. A sleeping giant could get killed. You hear me? If Trinidad is a giant, it must have its eyes wide open. Giant? You can't even get running water in your house. Every minute, water gone. What this country need is a Indian Prime Minister. We black people can't rule. All we know how to do is fête. You don't see Indian fêting like that. Is only when they have Hoosay or Phagwa. And is we black people who cause that. But a Indian would never start a fête just so. They mean business. All they think about is business. You know who really mash up this country? Is Eric Williams. I say Eric Williams mash up this country bad, bad, bad. I don't care if they lock me up for saying that. This is a free country. If I think Eric Williams mash up this country, I free to say that. And who don't like it, crapaud smoke their pipe. Is Eric Williams who mash up this country. You know what I mean. Before Eric Williams, if you didn't get some degree, you could never make any money. Now a plumber, a electrician making more money than a man with a degree. Where you ever see that? So how you expect the children to want to study hard and get all kind o' degree, if plumber and mechanic making so much money? And another thing with we black people, black man always thinking how he could get somebody wife. You never see a Indian do that. I have a partner always coming home by me and drinking up all meh liquor. He think I ain't know that is meh wife he want. But I waiting for him. I will castrate his behind. You never see a Indian do that. And a next thing again. Eric say it ain't have no Indian or Negro in this country, but only Trinny. Don't bother with that. Go down Caroni and say that! And when it come to food, you can't compete with a Indian. Because they didn't forget their food from India. They eat their own food. The Africans forget their food from Africa and now eating junk. But I tell you something. The sweetest woman in the world is a Dougla. You hear what the calypsonian say? A Dougla is six o' one, half a dozen o' the other. Half Indian, half Negro. So a Dougla woman is the best of both worlds. You can't ask for nothing nicer than a Dougla woman. And believe me, I know what I talking 'bout!'

Prior to that ride in Tony's taxi, Rufus had heard visitors to Auntie Mavis's house speak about Tony – sometimes with derision, but sometimes almost with reverence. There were those who described him as an orator *manqué*, a taxi-driver with an inborn talent for public speaking. He was noted for seizing the opportunity to practise his craft the minute the first passenger entered the taxi. In a tone that was impassioned without being strident, he articulated controversial, unpopular, provocative views. He didn't mind if those he provoked didn't respond. He didn't care if nobody paid attention. Rarely did a regular rider make the mistake of engaging him in debate. In any event, his self-sustaining monologues flowed easily without the need for comment from the truly 'captive' passengers. He himself supplied the answers to what were mostly rhetorical questions, all the while taking his hands off the steering-wheel and gesticulating, to the alarm of the passengers. Only a few minor road accidents had been directly caused by him.

The anecdotes Auntie Mavis heard about Tony made her torment herself with doubts. Was there something she should have done differently? Were there steps that could have been taken years earlier to prevent Tony from ever embarking on what now seemed to be an unstoppable course towards insanity? Had she shown the children enough love, in equal doses?

In fairness to Auntie Mavis, it must be said that she had tried hard to be even-handed and not show partiality or favouritism either in meting out punishment or in doling out treats. She also tried to foster a family spirit and, whether they liked it or not, she demanded group participation in certain family outings. However much Pearl and Tony professed to hate going to the beach, Auntie Mavis always insisted that they all go together – which they did on at least one Sunday afternoon every month.

Their most frequent destination used to be Carenage, and that involved a relatively short trip. For that reason, the children were greatly surprised one Saturday morning by the announcement that they would be setting out for a different beach at the break of dawn on Sunday. The name of the beach was not disclosed, but the sight of the enormous picnic lunch that Auntie Mavis started preparing gave them to understand that they were in for quite an expedition. Soon after she returned from the 5 o'clock mass the next morning, they were on their way.

Having fallen into a deep sleep until long after they had taken a road northwards from Arima, Rufus awoke to hear Auntie Mavis praising the scenery and the beauty of the local flora:

'There is no other place on earth where you will find a forest so beautiful. Only in Trinidad!'

Tony, who was still peeved that he had been dragooned into making a long, boring trip, mumbled that it was a jungle like any other jungle. What to Tony was just jungle was to Auntie Mavis a lush growth of beautiful tropical vegetation, and she kept telling the occupants of the car how beautiful it all was, to the point where Rufus, too, began to get bored. With an air of mischief, he took it upon himself to ask for the names of the different species that she found so beautiful.

'What's that tree with those things growing out of the trunk?'

'That's a cocoa-tree,' she replied. 'The things growing out of the trunk are the pods.'

'What are those pretty flowers over there and all over the place?'

'Those are the balisier palms. They are the symbol of the People's National Movement. Dr Williams was a real genius to think of that. A beautiful symbol!'

Those, however, were the easy questions, and eventually Rufus had the roguish satisfaction of seeing Auntie Mavis stumped when asked to give the specific names not only of some tall trees with twisted trunks, but also of the mosses and ferns covering their branches.

'Not even a plant scientist could name all the plants in Trinidad,' she admitted with humility.

As they entered yet another hamlet, she fell silent, the better to concentrate on avoiding dozing dogs and grazing goats. A few hamlets back, she had narrowly missed a hen that was nonchalantly escorting her chicks across the road.

After more forests of bamboo, balisier and nameless bush, there came the smell and sound of the sea. Auntie Mavis braked abruptly at a bend in the road, and Rufus at first thought the car had a flat tyre or some mechanical problem. Then he noticed in the waist-high bush a slight parting that revealed a footpath descending to a beach. The directions she had been following must have been perfect.

'You have to be careful,' Auntie Mavis warned. 'The ground is slippery and I don't want anybody falling down the hill. And look out for the razor grass. I don't want you to get cut. We'll have to make several trips to take everything down. Rufus will stay on the beach and watch our things. Let's move!'

Indeed the footpath was steep and treacherous. It looked as though it was not travelled too often, but often enough to prevent the hardiest of the encroaching weeds from recovering the whole territory for the bush. It was no easy matter to avoid the nettles, thorns and razor grass as they negotiated the track in single file with their assortment of picnic baskets, hampers, bags and bottles.

'Why did we have to bring so much food?' Rufus asked. 'And so much ice!'

The good thing about being appointed food-guard was that he wouldn't have to clamber up the track until it was time to go home. Yet while he welcomed the appointment, he didn't see the need for a food-guard. Not even a stray dog was in sight. Rushing up to tickle his toes as he stood at the water's edge, the foaming surf was his sole companion. It thus offered forceful testimony to the violence of the waves, for they broke at least a quarter of a mile out to sea on the rocks that rose up out of the water and formed a broken-toothed barrier ringing the bay. None but the tiniest of fishing boats would have been able to come in.

On that first visit to Blanchisseuse, Auntie Mavis embarrassed Rufus – not by anything she said or did to him, simply by gutting and filleting fish. To his mind, those were not things that anyone of Auntie Mavis's stature should be seen doing in public.

By 2 o'clock, that which had once seemed over-abundant had been devoured, and Tony was just beginning to relax and romp with Rufus in the mid-afternoon sun. To their great annoyance, Auntie Mavis picked that moment to announce that they would have to leave soon, because she wanted to stop at the Blanchisseuse fish market.

'For what?' Tony and Rufus protested.

'For fish.'

What was the point in arguing that people were selling fish all over Trinidad – and a lot closer to home?

'The fish up here is really fresh,' she had them know. 'You could see the fishermen bringing it in.'

And so it was.

Much to Rufus's chagrin, Auntie Mavis engaged in unbecoming haggling over the price of king fish and red fish. She got her way, too, shrugging off the fishermen's contention that the asking price included the cost of gutting:

'I'll gut it myself.'

And so she did, thereby managing to compound Rufus's mortification. Still, as he sat moping in the car, the full logic of Auntie Mavis's actions dawned on him. She had thought of everything: if she had prepared such a massive quantity of food, it was only because she had anticipated the appetite-stimulating power of the beach; if she had filled a cooler with ice, it was to ensure that enough was left over to pack the fish.

From Rufus's earliest memories of Auntie Mavis, she had been that way, always thinking of everything. So, obviously, she had planned the trip with meticulous precision; she had known exactly where to stop the car; she had not found the beach by sheer chance.

'How did you know about that beach? Did you ever go there before?' he asked as they started driving back through the cocoa plantations.

The question intrigued him and had been persisting in his head for the greater part of the day. But to pose it now was to make a pre-emptive strike and forestall any further ecstatic effusions from Auntie Mavis concerning the flora.

It was a messenger in her office who had told her about it. All along the north coast, he said, there were short stretches of beach tucked between cliffs that dropped straight down into the sea. Most were visible only from the air and accessible only from the sea. But the locals had found ways of getting to some of the most inaccessible. The messenger often spoke of one such beach which he continued to frequent. To him it was a beach made by God for the safety of children, a beach where, at low tide, a small child could walk out to the offshore rocks on which the waves smothered themselves. As a token of his special regard for Mavis, he revealed to her the ancestral village secret of access – but with a warning:

'It is the safest beach in the world, but we don't want the world to know about it. If the tourists discover it, they will kill it.'

There was no danger of that. Or at least, if it was going to be killed, the killers were likely to be the Lintons; the secluded, pristine beach became a Linton family retreat after Mavis shared the secret with her brothers and sisters. The first time she returned, she was able to squeeze Carmen and her son Patrick into the car, along with Tony, Pearl and Rufus. Again it meant leaving immediately after the 5 o'clock mass for the trip through the forests and past the occasional tethered goat, a trip that proved not so long and boring for Tony, but too long and tiring for young Patrick. Carmen spent a lot of time voicing her fears about letting the children go into the water, and reminding her sister that three children had drowned at Maracas the week before. Every so often, the sight of a clump of balisier would cause Mavis to mutter 'Eric Williams was a real genius', and that in turn would prompt an understanding nod from Rufus. But all the while, he was bedevilled by the prospect that too early in the afternoon he might be wrenched away from the frolicking with his cousins on the beach to the haggling with fish vendors, and that prospect diminished the joy that accompanied his anticipation.

Indeed it was far too early in the afternoon when, as feared, Auntie Mavis tried to round up the frolickers, but Rufus had his brilliant suggestion ready to be uttered:

'Why don't you leave Tony and Pearl here with us?'

It wasn't a bad idea, Mavis had to admit. Surely Tony and Pearl were responsible enough to supervise Patrick and Rufus, especially on such a safe beach. Carmen, however, would have none of it, and kept saying 'You never know what might happen', no doubt still haunted by visions of children drowning at Maracas. Moreover, upon their arrival in the morning, there had been an omen: the fact that young Patrick had tumbled out of the car and on to the ground accentuated his mother's fears that misfortune of greater dimensions lurked ahead. From Rufus's point of view, the greatest misfortune was that he was forced to relive the mortifying experience of seeing Auntie Mavis haggling with fish vendors.

It was obvious that Carmen was worried primarily about Patrick's safety. It seemed to Rufus that in all her waking hours, and maybe even in her sleep, she worried about Patrick. Rufus knew that despite Auntie Mavis's attempts to be even-handed, he was her favourite. Yet he was nagged by the feeling that a certain ingredient was missing from the love Auntie Mavis had for him. He had noticed how over-protective his other aunts were towards their children. He had seen how Carmen distressed herself whenever Patrick fell or had any kind of mishap. There was the time when Patrick tormented Rufus's dog Twinkle until she bit him. Carmen was sick with worry for weeks, looking for symptoms of rabies in her son – despite the assurances of Mavis, who knew the dog was not rabid, and those of the doctor, who had further distressed Carmen by giving the boy an injection. In the end, Mavis, for the sake of peace and quiet, had even promised, without meaning it, to have the dog destroyed. 'It might attack and kill somebody,' Carmen insisted. When she realized that Twinkle had been given a definitive reprieve, she sulked and kept away from Mavis's house.

For Rufus, that excess of concern was the highest expression of love. To be sure, Auntie Mavis was concerned about him, but in a more relaxed way, not with Carmen's intensity. Such intensity, he told himself, must be reserved for true, natural mothers; the love Auntie Mavis had for him couldn't be the real thing; after all, she wasn't his real mother.

The weekend arrived, and he was still keeping himself in solitary confinement. On Saturday afternoon, his friend Sally came to visit him. They hadn't seen each other, or spoken, since their conversation about her grandfather's will. Rufus had refused to accept her calls.

'So I see you have made your decision. At least you should have the courage to notify me,' Sally said.

'Decision on what?' asked Rufus, who had had little time to think about the implications of the Inspector's will. Sally reminded him of the revelation that her grandfather had fathered a child by Mrs Judith Linton. In the light of what Rufus had since learned, it was clear that the child had been Carmen, not Mavis, as he had earlier supposed. That changed little as far as Rufus and Sally were concerned. They were still very closely related by blood.

Rufus, for his part, brought Sally up to date. He explained to her why he so desperately wanted to talk to Carmen. It was certainly not love that he expected from her after some twenty years. Carmen could not now become the mother he had never had. It was far too late for that. He gave up hoping for a mother when he was about six. But he had always been able to identify a particular man as his father – a man who had had no time for Rufus, but whom Rufus had none the less considered, from a distance, with a sense of possession and admiration. Clive, the cricketing encyclopaedia boasting of his physical incapacity to get drunk and predicting how long it was going to rain, was *his* father. Of that he had been certain. But now, at one fell swoop, he had lost the father he knew and admired, and had been saddled with a mother he did not particularly care for.

'If it's the last thing I do in this life,' he told Sally, 'I have to follow this thing wherever it leads me. Whether my father is a priest or a murderer, I want to know.'

'What a morbid thought,' Sally responded with a half-giggle.

'It's not a giggling matter,' Rufus said sternly. 'And it would help explain why they have all acted in this way.'

'But how will you find out?' asked Sally, serious again.

'I'm going to confront her and ask her to her face. I must find out what is what and who is who.'

'I don't like the feel of this,' said Sally. 'This whole business makes me very uneasy.'

It was the day after Good Friday. Rufus didn't bother to telephone. He woke up early and decided: he was going to the house in Cascade. Dennis was certain to be either in a betting parlour or at the Union Park racecourse for the opening day of the Easter meeting. He was more likely to be at the racecourse, with Patrick. He would not have been deterred by the length of the journey from Cascade or by the nation-wide gasoline shortage. He tried not to miss any of the important meetings in the racing calendar. He followed the horses even to Tobago, and Patrick followed him every time.

Dennis was the only person Rufus knew who spent hours reading horse-racing magazines and poring over pictures of thoroughbreds. Having investigated arcane aspects of breeding, feeding and training, he would look at the neck of a horse and tell Patrick whether it was a sprinter or a stayer. His collection of racing statistics helped him to develop a partiality towards one trainer/jockey combination: a horse trained by Harper and ridden by Griffith always had his money. He familiarized himself with the body weight of jockeys, their career wins, and the career records of horses. He would instruct Patrick as to who the best apprentice jockeys were; which jockeys worked magic with their mounts; which horses were capable of taking top weight and still having the class and the speed to defeat a strong field; which horses had the stamina to stay on well at the finish after sustaining good early speed; which horses loved to chase the leaders into the straight and then quicken in the closing stages; which horses ran creditably only over the sprint distances; and which horses consistently showed their best form when encountering sloppy track conditions. Nothing, however, was permitted to obscure the vital question: whether to place a straight bet or do some kind of permutation or combination.

When all was studied and deliberated, Dennis didn't just rely on his knowledge of the reputations of horses, jockeys, trainers, owners and breeders. He also took the advice of his young son. If Patrick liked the sound of a horse's name, he picked it to win. Sometimes, his hunch paid off. Sometimes, too, by some fluke, he correctly predicted the horses finishing first, second and third. Though his mother had an appropriate dose of admiration for his father's horse expertise, it was not uncommon for her to drop the remark that Patrick had the special power of a good-luck charm. It was also a fact that Carmen had her own reasons for insisting that Patrick always accompany his father to the races. She felt confident that Dennis, with Patrick at his heels, would not be lured away from the horses by any enchantress.

As expected, neither Dennis nor Patrick was at home. What Rufus had not expected was to be shown into the living-room by Carmen without even a hint of protest or surprise. She lit up a cigarette and offered him one. That made him uncomfortable. He had never seen her smoking, never even known her to be a smoker. The cigarette, he thought, made her look cheap – like a cheap actress in a second-rate film. He didn't want to be part of that scene, and refused the cigarette.

'My nerves are settled enough,' he said.

She did not even smile.

'So what are you going to do with your latest discovery?' she asked. 'You can't blackmail me, you know. There are no secrets between my husband and me.'

'It's not money I want. And if I wanted money, you would have to beat me to get me to steal yours.'

This time she smiled:

'I see we have a real smarty-pants bastard on our hands.'

'At least you didn't call me a son of a bitch,' Rufus retorted.

'Look, Rufus. This is starting off all wrong. I have nothing against you, and you can't make me feel guilty.'

'I'm not trying to make you feel guilty. But if you had any kind of human feeling, you would feel guilty. Not because you had a child without being married. To me that is not a crime. But you carried on a pretence for years, and made me feel as if I dropped from a tree and didn't belong to anybody. *That* is the crime. How do you think I felt as a child growing up?'

'In the first place,' Carmen replied, 'the pretence wasn't my idea, but your grandmother's. Besides, you think it's easy to feel guilty for twenty years. After a while, you just have to try not to think about things.'

𝄢 𝄢 𝄢

Rufus picked himself up from the kitchen floor. He saw that there was a lot of blood everywhere, blood on his hands, blood on his clothes, blood on the floor, blood on a kitchen knife on the floor. He saw Carmen on the floor. He bent down to study her face. It was fixed in a look, not of terror, but rather of disbelief. It appeared to him to be a face of stone, an unfriendly, forbidding face that had never been capable of reflecting tender sentiments. The heart, he was sure, must have been exactly like the face. But that was only his perception. How was he to know what sort of heart she had? With a wry smile, he whispered in her ear 'Mummy', and was immediately self-conscious. He thought he looked grotesque, though there was no one around to see.

He telephoned the police then went into the bathroom. He opened the tap to wash his hands, thought better of it, went into Carmen's bedroom, and decided to wait there for the police.

He wondered what was taking them so long. His call to 999 must have sounded like a hoax. 'I think I have killed a woman,' he had said. The operator hadn't responded until he had repeated his words. 'Give me your name and address,' she had finally said.

He could have given a false name. He could have run away. But he could not abandon Carmen now; he wanted to stay with the body. Suppose the police never came? He could picture Dennis and Patrick returning from their day at the races and finding him hanging around with blood all over his hands, while Carmen lay dead on the floor. Patrick would surely scream for help. Dennis might hang his head and weep. They would think Rufus a murderer.

He was convinced that he was, but he still couldn't remember. He got into bed, Carmen's bed, between the sheets, and fell asleep.

A policeman in uniform was shaking him. It was not too rough a shake, Rufus thought. Not too rough, considering.

'What took you so long?' Rufus asked. The policeman looked puzzled.

'You better be careful what you say. You are under arrest.'

Those were not quite the words Rufus was expecting to hear. He had seen and read so many arrest scenes. The policeman was supposed to warn him that anything he said might be used in evidence against him. He felt like pointing that out to the policeman, but decided not to. Another policeman was standing by the bedroom door, saying nothing. Rufus could hear footsteps in other parts of the house, heavy footsteps of men wearing heavy boots and trying not to make a commotion. They spoke in soft tones.

'You have the murderer cornered like a rat,' Rufus said, with an exaggerated sense of melodrama. 'Do you think he'll try to get out of the trap?'

The policeman said nothing.

They didn't bother to handcuff Rufus. He would have been most offended if they had. That would have implied a measure of mistrust that was totally uncalled for. After all, he had waited patiently for them to come and arrest him. On the steps of Police Headquarters, he turned round and, pointing to the Red House, said:

'That is where it all started.'

On hearing the news, Mrs Judith Linton first became hysterical in her distress. She bawled for mercy and called on the Lord to take her and send her to hell as punishment for the shame and misfortune she had brought on the family. The doctor had to sedate her. Then she went into a state of shock, and they had to call the doctor back. The other members of the family were no less devastated by the news. They began to congregate at Mavis's house later the same evening. The grim question on everyone's mind was how it could have happened. Carmen had never been popular with her brothers and sisters. They had found her cold and stuck-up. She used to have a way of giving unsolicited advice, of implying that her in-laws were not good enough for the Linton family, of insisting that her son Patrick was far more mannerly than any of his cousins. For some time, she hadn't been on speaking terms with Clive, for whom she had professed a great and irreversible hatred. Her brothers and sisters had all had occasional misgivings about keeping Rufus in the dark on the question of his mother's identity. Clive for one felt that she had proved unappreciative and unworthy of the efforts they had made to spare her embarrassment. But none of them had ever dreamed that it would come to this, that she would end up being stabbed to death by her own unacknowledged son.

The evening had many of the appearances of a wake, even though it hadn't been planned as such and the corpse was absent. Graham and Cecil, the two youngest boys, began a fittingly mournful rendition of 'Abide with me'. Mavis and her sister Linda brought out lots of coffee and biscuits. Clive helped himself to rum, and before long, retired to a corner to sob into his glass. But it was he who raised the question that had remained taboo all evening:

'What are we to do about Rufus?'

'Let him hang!' Cecil replied without hesitation.

Indeed the majority view, at first, was that the family should stand aside and let the full force of the law fall upon Rufus. The only dissenters were Clive and Mavis.

'We are all to blame for what has happened,' she argued. 'We didn't do too well by Rufus before now. The least we can do now is see to it that he gets a good lawyer.'

'I don't see why we should help our sister's murderer get away scot-free,' Cecil countered.

'We shouldn't be calling the boy a murderer,' Clive noted. 'That is for the court to decide.'

The argument went on for a while and, in the end, the avengers decided to go along with the dissenters. The family would not abandon Rufus. They would seek out the best defence lawyer they could afford, and would share the costs.

The following day, Easter Sunday, Auntie Mavis went to visit Rufus. He greeted her with tearful apologies.

'I'm sorry I disappointed you, Auntie. I just don't know what came over me. You must all be ashamed of me.'

Mavis was consoling in her tone. She felt, however, that now was not the time for consolation. With her practical mind, she was more concerned about protecting Rufus.

'What have you told the police?' she asked.

'I told them that I probably killed her.'

'Probably?'

'I don't see how anyone else could have done it. But I don't remember doing it. I must have had a blackout.'

Mavis frowned intensely. She could foresee difficulties with that line of defence. She was also somewhat disturbed by the attitude Rufus appeared to be taking. He spoke as one who would willingly condemn himself, spurn all attempts to save him, and reject all offers of clemency. She wasn't clinging to the false hope that somebody else might have entered the house and killed Carmen. But there were such things as diminished responsibility, extenuating circumstances, even self-defence. Surely a good lawyer could think of something plausible.

'We are trying to get Nozick to take your case,' Auntie Mavis said. 'Your Uncle Clive knows a solicitor who is a good friend of Nozick's. We think we can arrange it. Uncle Clive is going to his house today.'

Rufus was taken aback, and began to utter a protest:

'You can't afford Nozick. He will take away your house and land, and I will still hang.'

'You must not talk like that,' Mavis pleaded. 'You are entitled to a fair trial. Before they can do anything to you, a jury will have to find you guilty.'

'I don't know if I can survive a trial, unless they make it very, very brief. I plead guilty, the jury agrees, and the judge orders them to hang me by the neck until dead. How about that?'

They were both silent for a moment, then Mavis said:

'If we can't get Nozick, we'll try to get Harkness.'

Rufus began to sing:

I done tell meh friends and meh family, not to worry.
Anyone o' them interfere with me, take it easy.
Don't worry to beg the jury. Save the lawyer fee.
But if you have any mail, send it to me at the Royal Gaol.

Auntie Mavis recognized the tune. It had been one of Sparrow's hits some time in the early 1960s, she seemed to remember. A smile forced itself to her face. Rufus had always been a Sparrow fan and used to entertain the household with his performances. He had the ability to remember the melody and lyrics of a calypso after hearing it only a couple of times. He had capitalized on that ability at primary school. Once, during a geography lesson, he had been flogged in front of the class for transcribing the words of one of the naughty Sparrow calypsos, for sale to his classmates.

'It will be a waste of time and money to get me an expensive lawyer,' Rufus said. 'Save the lawyer fee.'

The family did manage to retain Nozick, who visited Rufus two days later. Rufus had never before seen him in the flesh, though he had seen his picture in the papers. He was known to be a formidable defence lawyer, and it was commonly said that in seven years he had amassed a fortune by winning the acquittal of murder suspects. In reference to him, words such as 'gifted', 'tenacious', 'disarming' and 'persuasive' were bandied about. His fame had travelled throughout the land and even to some of the neighbouring islands. As Rufus set eyes on the strapping six-footer, he was deeply impressed by the mere physical aspect of the man. He had often visualized lawyers as little, weasel-faced, bespectacled ferrets, just waiting to snap at the witnesses, trip them up, get them all confused. This giant of a man, stature equalling reputation, appeared capable of cowing the prosecution witnesses into submission by simply standing up. But his voice was a disappointment. Where Rufus had expected a deep, captivating, resonant boom, he heard a grating squeak that seemed to emanate from a less imposing figure.

'What's the point of all that? I don't want this thing to drag on forever!' Rufus interjected, as Nozick began explaining that there would first be a preliminary hearing to determine if the evidence was sufficient for Rufus to be put on trial. 'It's all a waste of time. Can't you waive it or speed it up?'

It sounded more like a plea than a demand. Nozick looked at Rufus and wondered. But he understood; he would see what he could do to expedite the proceedings. He didn't at all enjoy what Rufus had to say about Carmen's death, but he tried not to betray any signs of disbelief. His policy was to give his clients the benefit of the doubt. He would pretend to believe even if he sensed that they were lying. If they had a story all worked out, he wouldn't try to change it. He assured them that he would build their defence on what they told him. But he would let them know that they couldn't change their story once the trial began, without risk of losing their case. His general attitude often induced them to 'come clean' – before the trial began.

He had never had a client who claimed to have blacked out while committing the crime of which he was accused. He had heard of similar cases in other countries, but doubted that such a claim would convince the average Trinidadian juror, especially when the charge was matricide. Only a handful of his previous clients had openly admitted guilt at the outset. On the contrary, most of them had begun by protesting total innocence. At the very least, they had been anxious to justify their acts and emphasize any extenuating circumstances. Rufus was saying that he had killed Carmen, but could not remember doing so. It was going to be a tough one to argue.

In the weeks that followed, Nozick was to learn a great deal about Rufus, his childhood disappointments, his longing for a mother, his discoveries. But Rufus's account of the events on the fateful Saturday in Cascade never changed. In the end, Nozick truly believed. With some help from Auntie Mavis and her contacts, he managed to have an early date set for the preliminary examination. It would not be an exaggeration to describe the committal proceedings as perfunctory. There was no astonishment when Rufus was committed for trial – in mid-October, soon after the start of the new law term. It was an answer to Rufus's prayer that he wouldn't have to join the crowd and sit around in prison for ever, awaiting trial. It was also a tribute to Auntie Mavis. She again showed that, once she decided it was right to pull strings for her family, she was capable of hauling rope. If only, she thought, he had asked her to see about his passport from the outset, he might now be settling down to his studies overseas, instead of preparing to stand trial for murder.

About a week before the trial opened, Nozick surprised Rufus by asking him:

'Do you own a suit?'

'I wouldn't be caught dead in one,' Rufus replied.

'I'll remember to tell them when they hang you.'

Auntie Mavis, too, started putting pressure on Rufus to wear a suit at the trial. The question of suits was a long-standing bone of contention between the two. He had never once worn the suit she had bought him on his 18th birthday – that is to say, he had never worn the two pieces together. He had worn the jacket at funerals, as a mark of respect. Now she insisted on buying him a three-piece suit for his trial.

'You can't do yourself any harm by looking presentable,' she said.

The Red House, Again

Certainly the policemen who escorted him to the First Assize Court looked presentable, with their impeccable grooming and neat white jackets. So did the trial judge as he strode regally into the room. The lapels on his billowing gown continued down the entire length of the garment, but for a second, Rufus had the impression that he had draped a long scarf round his neck. In deference, all stood silently, and some bowed. When the judge sat down, he was visible to Rufus from only the neck up, exhibiting one of those perpetually smiling faces that seemed too frail and avuncular to be stern.

The courtroom atmosphere was strange to Rufus. It wasn't just the solemnity and the formality; it was also the realization that he was up against a mighty power residing far away and originating further beyond – the power of the Crown. He had no quarrel with the Crown. He used to join in lustily when Auntie Mavis used to play 'God Save the Queen' on the piano. Later on, she had added local patriotic songs to her repertoire. With requisite enthusiasm, he had learned those too. Then there he was, three weeks before his 7th birthday, parroting the words of the new national anthem on the night the Union Jack was lowered.

He was filled with a sense of strangeness now, on hearing that it was the Crown versus Rufus Linton, the Crown versus him! No matter. He still knew the words to 'God Save the Queen'.

'May it please Your Lordship, Mr Foreman and members of the jury,' the Senior Crown Counsel intoned, 'the accused stands accused of the offence of murder.'

The Senior Crown Counsel was a smirker, all oozing with confidence. You could see he felt he had the case all wrapped up, even against the formidable Nozick with his fabled powers of persuasion. He told the jury of their responsibility to the country and the accused, and said 'You will hear … ' dozens of times. Rufus was all spruced up and feeling ridiculous in his three-piece suit. But the sight of the gowns and wigs worn by the judges and the lawyers made it easier for him. He started taking notes, but, during a recess, Nozick told him that note-taking would make him look indifferent and detached, and lose him any sympathy the jurors might have for him. It would do him little good to appear cool and unconcerned during the proceedings.

Rufus felt neither indifferent nor detached, neither cool nor unconcerned. He had no doubt what the verdict would be. But it was his life that was at stake, and he was keenly interested in every aspect of the proceedings. He may have looked unruffled, but he was deeply offended, on that first day, by the Senior Crown Counsel's opening remarks; he had been depicted as a totally heartless, ungrateful and cold-blooded man. The Senior Crown Counsel had promised to prove to the jury 'beyond any conceivable suspicion of doubt that the prisoner did carefully and deliberately plan and carry out his wilful act of murder at Cascade on the afternoon of the 29th of March 1975, by stabbing a defenceless woman to death with a kitchen knife'. Rufus had had to restrain himself. He had wanted to shout out, for all to hear, that the Senior Crown Counsel was misrepresenting the facts. He had promised himself to set the record straight when they put him in the witness-box.

Nozick's opening remarks impressed Rufus, although he was slightly bothered by the high-pitched squeak. He promised to tell the court about the pattern of deception used to fool Rufus over the years. He would show how that deception had denied Rufus the true sense of identity that normally leads to emotional stability; how he had been dealt a succession of cruel and devastating blows; how he had been led to believe that a certain man was his father; how all of a sudden he had been told it was not so; how he still did not know who his father was; how he had been led to believe that his mother was far away, living in Venezuela; how all of a sudden he had been told that she had been in close proximity all along; how those developments had placed Rufus under severe psychological and emotional stress, and eventually caused a breakdown.

Rufus was moved by the power of Nozick's oratory, and tried to determine if the jurors were too. It was hard to tell. They all looked so grim and stone-faced. Their stone faces became even grimmer when they heard the testimony of the police inspector who had gone to the house on the day of the alleged murder.

'Where did you find the accused?' asked the Senior Crown Counsel.

'In the dead woman's bed,' replied the inspector.

The Senior Crown Counsel reflectively fingered his winged collars, perhaps making sure they were still properly secured with the white bands. He obviously wanted to dwell on the bedroom scene.

'Would you be so kind as to tell the court what the accused was doing in the dead woman's bed?'

'He was sleeping, sir.'

One juror could not restrain herself, and her gasp was heard throughout the courtroom. In the public gallery, several mouths tut-tutted in disapproving disbelief. Were Rufus's eyes playing tricks on him, or did he indeed descry in the gallery the roving protester he had first seen in another section of the Red House? A second look convinced him. No one could be mistaken for her. There couldn't be another emaciated woman in all of Trinidad with that combination of a snub nose, bony features and gold teeth. How extraordinary that she could sit still and remain intent on the proceedings for so long! She must have been under sedation.

'In all my years of experience in dealing with such matters,' the Senior Crown Counsel was saying, 'I have never encountered such a remorseless, cold-blooded reaction by a murderer.'

Nozick immediately lifted his burly frame to shout: 'I strongly object, My Lord.' Of course, the objection was upheld by the judge, who by now had slipped deeper into his seat. For that reason, his lips couldn't be seen by Rufus and his utterances seemed to come from his wig.

The word 'remorseless' troubled Rufus, increasing the burden of his repressed awareness that he felt far less remorse than he should have. He could see that the Senior Crown Counsel's words were not erased from the jurors' minds, even when Nozick, during the cross-examination, so shrewdly put another interpretation on the actions of the accused.

'Why did the police go to the house on the 29th of March?' Nozick asked.

'A telephone call came in to 999 about a killing at the house.'

'Do you know who made the call?'

'The accused, sir.'

'Do you know how long after the call was received you and your men arrived at the house?'

'I do not know, sir,' replied the inspector, somewhat sheepishly.

'Do you know at what time you got to the house?'

'Yes, sir. We arrived at approximately 5.40 p.m.'

'The records show that the call was received by the 999 oper-ator at approximately 3.25 p.m.'

The inspector said nothing.

'You and your men,' Nozick said, 'reached the house more than two hours after the accused telephoned 999.'

'We went as soon as we were dispatched,' protested the inspector.

'The police are not on trial here,' Nozick assured him. 'You have not been charged with undue delay in responding to calls. The point is that the accused waited more than two hours for you to arrive. He made absolutely no attempt to leave the house.'

'He still had no right to be in her bed,' the inspector mumbled.

'You are not here to lecture us on the rights of the accused,' Nozick said sternly. And the judge joined in with a warning to the witness to confine himself to answering the questions.

But, again, Rufus could sense the impact of the inspector's words. The jurors seemed almost to be nodding in agreement with the inspector that Rufus had no right to be in Carmen's bed.

'The accused,' said Nozick, 'had reached a state of total emotional, psychological and physical exhaustion. He was completely drained and disoriented. He was aware that some great tragedy had occurred, but was incapable, totally incapable, of comprehending the event. He collapsed into a bed – it could have been the floor, the sofa, the child's bed – he collapsed and waited for help to arrive. All his life this motherless child had been crying for help, and he was again crying for help on that fateful day.'

'Now my learned friend is the one getting carried away and lecturing to us,' the Senior Crown Counsel popped up to inter-ject. 'What kind of cross-examination is this?'

Somewhere in the gallery, somebody snickered.

Rufus wasn't happy with Nozick's interpretation, which he found too clinical. He was just as unhappy with the testimony of Nozick's surprise witness, whose arrival caused a minor sensation. Even the sensational weeklies, which usually were tipped off about such events, were taken by surprise. Of course few laymen would have heard of Professor Martinez, but the rumour – later discounted – that he was an American brought down, at the expense of the defence, specially for the trial could have been played up, and would have helped to sell a few more copies. The reporters were not to be denied, however; they had a field-day when the Senior Crown Counsel crossed swords with the Professor.

Professor Martinez started well. He looked and sounded self-assured and authoritative. At Nozick's request, he told the court that he was born in Trinidad, had once lived in the United States, and had studied, treated and written books and articles about amnesiacs. Rufus's case, he stated, was not unusual. He had encountered stable and well-adjusted individuals who had experienced single episodes of amnesia, brought on by severe emotional stress. Some of them had become patients of his. Some had been charged with crimes they did not remember committing.

'How would you explain,' Nozick asked, 'the action of the accused in lying on his mother's bed?'

'A return to the womb,' replied the Professor.

'Go on. Please elaborate.'

'One has to bear in mind that Rufus has always been emotionally deprived. He was never given a chance to enjoy any of that natural closeness between mother and child. In his state of emotional collapse, he still yearned for that intimacy. In approaching the bed, he was, for once, approaching his mother's arms. In getting into bed, he was getting into her arms and, in a manner of speaking, returning to her womb.'

Nozick began to feel uneasy. He knew that the jury wasn't impressed, and almost regretted asking the Professor to elaborate. Perhaps it had been a mistake to call him to the witness-box. The jury was clearly not receptive to his pedagogical drone.

'We have all heard,' said the Senior Crown Counsel as he launched into his attack, 'of the mistakes, not to say misdeeds, of psychiatry in some countries. You people merely speculate, don't you?'

'There is an element of informed, intelligent theorizing involved in our work,' replied the Professor. 'But it is all founded on close observation and empirical data.'

'You use words and phrases which are unclear to me,' said the Senior Crown Counsel, playing with his winged collars in a more affected manner than before. 'For the benefit of those of us who are not experts in your field, would you care to express yourself in simpler terms? How sure are you that the accused did in fact suffer a loss of memory?'

'On the basis of my examination of the patient, and in my professional judgement, I have no doubt that he did in fact suffer a loss of memory.'

'You are referring to him as a patient. But is he sick? He doesn't appear sick to me.'

'In so far as he has experienced a significant psychological dysfunction, it is appropriate to qualify him as a patient.'

'How can you be sure,' asked the Senior Crown Counsel, 'that he didn't fake the whole thing?'

Nozick objected loudly, and before the judge could rule, the Senior Crown Counsel rephrased the question:

'How can you be sure that the accused didn't pretend to have suffered a loss of memory?'

Nozick again objected, but was overruled.

The Professor did not budge:

'Having looked carefully into all the circumstances of the case, there is no doubt in my mind that the patient, or the accused if you prefer, suffered a loss of memory on the day in question.'

'Would another expert in your field arrive at the same conclusion?' asked the Senior Crown Counsel.

'I believe so.'

'You believe so, but are you sure?'

'There can be no absolute guarantee of it, but I am sure that most experts would form the same conclusion.'

'But the majority could be wrong, couldn't they?' the Senior Crown Counsel suggested.

'All things are possible, but I believe the majority would be right.'

The Senior Crown Counsel suddenly turned his back on the witness and, staring straight at the jury, declared:

'We have had enough gobbledegook for one day. It is time to stop playing with words, Mr Professor. You know full well that your testimony could be contradicted on every single point by an equally qualified and distinguished professor. You claim that the accused suffered a loss of memory. Ten other professors would brand him a fake.'

He paused for a moment, then turned round and glared at the Professor:

'I have no further questions.'

Rufus was greatly relieved to see the Professor dismissed. He had tried in vain to dissuade Nozick from bringing any psychiatrist to the trial.

'I am not a madman,' Rufus had said.

'We know of a highly respected professor who has worked on cases like yours,' Nozick had replied.

In the end, convinced that psychiatrist or no psychiatrist, he would still be found guilty, and lacking the energy to argue with Nozick, Rufus had acquiesced.

The real argument between the two was on whether Rufus should give evidence in his own defence. Nozick had wrestled with the dilemma for weeks before the trial. He knew that juries tended to view as an admission of guilt the defendant's decision not to testify. But he felt that the defeatist, self-destructive streak in Rufus would make him his own worst witness. Rufus was adamant. He insisted on having his say in court.

Though the buzz of conversation across the country was still about the hanging of Abdul Malik a few months earlier, ghoulish preoccupation with the Linton trial was taking over. The crowd waiting outside the Red House to catch a glimpse of the accused had grown larger every morning, to the point where some commentators with long memories began saying that the case was generating almost as much interest as the trial of Boysie Singh. For a number of days running, food vendors did a brisk business in and around Woodford Square, and even on the balcony outside the courtroom. To no one's surprise, the public gallery was packed and attentive when Rufus entered the witness-box. There were quite a few faces he recognized, apart from that of the roving protester. Little Scobie was there – no doubt collecting material for a calypso, Rufus surmised. Indeed 'The Mighty Fledgeling' had finally managed to get a calypso recorded, and it was being given considerable air play. It was about a man named Boris who had walked into the French Embassy in Port-of-Spain claiming to be a KGB agent seeking asylum. As the calypso unfolded, it turned out that Boris could not speak a single word of Russian, and abused the Embassy staff in French patois; he had been born in Fyzabad and had a long history of delusions, once dressing up as a nun and entering the premises of a convent. Rufus found the calypso truly hilarious, and smiled knowingly at Little Scobie in an attempt to convey ecstatic approval.

Little Scobie's parents were there too, as were Miss Haynes and Zala Ngobi. For Rufus, scanning those faces was like briefly reviewing his odyssey from the time he had gone to the Red House to apply for his birth certificate. It took him a while to realize that even Mano from Tobago was in the courtroom. Maybe it was because he had always seen Mano wearing a large weather-beaten straw hat, to which he fondly referred as 'Geronimo my sombrero'. Without Geronimo, and wearing a suit instead of the plaid-shirt-and-dungarees uniform, Mano wasn't Mano. As Rufus thought about Geronimo the sombrero, he remembered an anecdote. Some years earlier, Mano, then an ambulance-driver at the Scarborough Hospital, had been sent to the home of a doctor to bring her back to attend to a very sick patient. As usual, he had sounded the horn. Somewhere in the house, the dogs had started barking, and he had waited in the ambulance. Not seeing the doctor emerge, he had gone up to the gate, provoking even fiercer barking, and had called out the doctor's name. A few minutes later, the doctor's husband, a well-known politician, had driven up to the gate, probably returning from some important meeting or function (Mano thought), for he was all dressed up and looking important. For a moment, Mano also thought that the doctor had accompanied him, but she was not in the car.

'Why are you creating such a brouhaha?' shouted the doctor's husband.

'With respect, sir,' said Mano, suspecting that a brouhaha was not a welcome creation, 'I am not creating nothing of the sort. I just came to take the doctor up to the hospital. A sick man up there waiting for her.'

'My advice to you is to go away,' said the doctor's husband, who then unlocked his gate, drove the car into his garage, returned to the gate to lock it, and again ordered Mano away.

Mano was a student of the Bible. He kept his copy in the ambulance, and in his spare time he would open it at random and lose himself in the text, in turn fascinated, awed, comforted. Often he would go directly to the Psalms, and soon he would be completely at peace with himself and the world. So frequently had he resorted to Psalm 23 for solace in all kinds of distressing situations that he knew it by heart. Almost instinctively, then, he started reciting it, as much to himself as for the benefit of the doctor's husband:

'The Lord is my shepherd; I shall not want ... Though I walk through the valley of the shadow of death, I will fear no evil ... Surely goodness and mercy shall follow me all the days of my life ... '

The recital failed to produce any discernible effect on the doctor's husband.

Mano took out the flask of rum he always carried for emergencies. The rum helped him to reflect on what was taking place. A man was dying at the hospital. The doctor might be able to do something to ease his suffering. She knew why the ambulance was there, but wouldn't even show her face. And the husband was just as indifferent; he was chasing the ambulance-driver away. It was more than Mano could bear. He sounded the horn again, and the dogs, still in the house, started barking again. Then, with rum-inspired courage, he went up to the gate and called on the doctor to come up to the hospital to save a man's life, 'if you have any feeling or mercy in your heart'. At that point, the doctor's husband let the dogs out of the house. They were four in number: a German Shepherd, a Retriever, a Bull Terrier and a Boxer. The malicious and the insensitive, pointing to the fact that the couple were childless, referred to the dogs as 'their four beloved children'. And how they would snigger when they heard the doctor say things like 'Now, don't be naughty, little darling Felicity' to the hideous-looking Boxer, the same Boxer which, according to a disgruntled former maid, used to curl up in bed with the doctor and her husband.

Felicity led the charge to the gate, causing Mano such a start that Geronimo his sombrero fell off his head and nearly landed on the wrong side of the gate. But Mano had his revenge. Casting aside Psalm 23, he resorted to a full range of expletives, hurling abuse at the dogs, accusing them of unspeakable acts with the doctor and her husband. The neighbours didn't have to strain their ears. The barking of the dogs was like a muted accompaniment to the swearing. 'You want brouhaha? I will create brouhaha in your backside,' he shouted. As the dogs barked on, he charged that the doctor had forgotten where she had come from. 'The bitch you call your mother used to sell fish in the market!' At the end of it all, came the peroration that was to be immortalized in the recounting of the incident:

'And to add insult to injury, you send your blasted beloved bloodhound children to bark at me and Geronimo my sombrero!'

Poor Mano. The hospital had fired him, and the drinking had got worse. But that had been years ago. The new Mano was a staunch teetotaller. Just to see him sitting in the public gallery and looking so grave in his suit brought a smile to Rufus's face. He was still smiling when it dawned on him that he was being called to the witness-box. Everyone was looking at him and probably wondering what he had to smile about. That had always been a problem for Rufus. His mind would stray from what was going on about him. He would smile – and sometimes even laugh out loud – at incidents, faces and anecdotes that came to mind. It was always such a nuisance when he was asked to explain why he was smiling, for the humour was seldom appreciated by those to whom he tried to explain. Thus the reward of shared amusement was rarely available to compensate him for the violation and exposure of such private moments of recollection. He could just imagine what the jurors were thinking about him, the alleged murderer smiling so broadly as he was about to testify.

Rufus experienced an intense feeling of surprise and disappointment when, after repeatedly scanning the faces in the gallery, he realized that Sally Johnson was not present, but he told himself that he shouldn't have been surprised. Her family had urged her to put as much distance as possible between Rufus and herself, especially after Nozick had raised the possibility of her appearing as a character witness. Nozick had concluded, however, that evidence of Rufus's good disposition or good moral character would do nothing to help the case for the defence.

The Senior Crown Counsel's cross-examination was in harrowing contrast to Nozick's gentle treatment. Nozick's questions Rufus had heard before. He had replied mechanically, in a matter-of-fact tone of voice, not trying to prove anything, fully convinced of the futility of Nozick's efforts, and showing his boredom with the whole trial. But when the Senior Crown Counsel demanded in slimy tones: 'Why did you go to the house that day?'; 'Did you have any hostile feelings towards your mother?'; 'Did you ever wish her dead?', Rufus had to wake up and take notice.

'How good is your memory?' was one of the Senior Crown Counsel's questions. Rufus paused to reflect. His memory wasn't bad. He had been particularly good at memorizing poems, and could still recite many he had learned as a child. So he replied:

'I have a very good memory.'

Nozick winced. The Senior Crown Counsel, slightly surprised at the ease with which he had elicited that admission, continued:

'So you would not describe yourself as the forgetful sort?'

'No, sir. I would not.'

'Would you describe yourself as the sort of person who conveniently forgets things?'

'No, sir. I would not.'

'Would you describe yourself as a violent person?'

'No, sir. I would not.'

'How do you react when you lose your temper?'

'I always try to control my temper,' Rufus replied.

'Do you remember the Sunday when you had to be forcibly restrained by your Uncle Clive?'

Rufus was taken aback. How on earth had the Senior Crown Counsel learned of that incident? Nozick intervened agitatedly to suggest that the Senior Crown Counsel's questions were irrelevant, but the judge allowed the line of questioning to proceed.

'Do you remember the Sunday when you began using profane language and breaking bottles in your aunt's house?'

Rufus was silent, and the Senior Crown Counsel repeated the question.

'I don't see what you are driving at,' Rufus said eventually.

'Do you remember being able to control your temper that Sunday?'

'I lost my temper,' Rufus acknowledged. 'It can happen to anyone.'

'We all lose our temper from time to time,' observed the Senior Crown Counsel, 'but not with such violence. And if we do become violent, it is not something we easily forget. Don't you agree?'

The judge told Rufus he didn't have to answer, and he didn't.

'You say you have a very good memory. You say you always try to control your temper. You can remember one recent occasion when you lost your temper and became violent. Yet you want us to believe that you have no recollection of that even more recent occasion on which you stabbed your mother to death. Mr Linton, you are blessed with a very selective memory.'

Nozick's closing speech had the entire court riveted. He gave a commanding performance and demonstrated to any doubters why he was always in demand as a defence lawyer. It was said that as president of a debating society in his student days, he had never lost a debate. He could pick a hole in any argument and drive his point home. All the same, towards the middle of the closing speech, Rufus spotted a juror in the second row nodding off intermittently, then looking around to see if anyone had noticed. At one point, only the whites of his eyes were visible in the sockets. His eyeballs appeared to roll around in his head, as the words 'absence of malice afore-thought', 'irresistible impulse' and 'mental irresponsibility' rolled off Nozick's tongue. In a few seconds he roused himself, to find Rufus staring at him, and, more defiant than embarrassed, he returned Rufus's gaze. Meanwhile, the other jurors were drinking in Nozick's words.

Rufus was relieved when it was all over. He was relieved that the whole process hadn't lasted too long. He was also relieved, and not in the least bit surprised, when he was found guilty. It was even something of an anti-climax. In his final words to the court, he asked those present not to harbour hostile feelings against him; maybe some day he would understand how and why he had done what he couldn't remember doing, but he wasn't making any excuses for himself; he deserved and would accept punishment.

The judge sat straight up. Assuming a stern and forbidding air with more help from his wig than from his face, he sentenced Rufus Linton to hang.

The Royal Gaol

Nozick was not the sort of lawyer ever to say die. Having reviewed the entire proceedings and spoken at length with his colleagues, he convinced himself and Auntie Mavis that there were substantial grounds for an appeal: the prosecution had failed to prove its case for wilful and deliberate murder, and the trial judge had omitted to direct the jurors on three crucial points – that they must believe the accused to have been of sound memory and discretion at the time of the occurrence, that they were free to exercise their best judgement in rejecting, either wholly or in part, confessional statements emanating from a weak or excited state of mind, that none of the statements made by Rufus amounted to a confession of his guilt. Nozick was confident that he would win eventually, even if it meant appealing all the way to the Privy Council. He was anxious to file the application for leave to appeal. It wouldn't drag on indefinitely, he assured Rufus. Hadn't he been able to expedite everything so far? But he doubted that Rufus had the stamina to go through with it. And he was right.

'Make sure the rope is good and sturdy,' Rufus said, not looking away from Nozick's string tie. 'I don't want them to have to do it twice.'

It had happened before. Some might have argued that any man with enough of a neck to break the rope should be allowed to live, by way of concession to the notion of divine intervention. Surely his time had not yet come. His maker was not ready for him. But the law of the land made no provision for eleventh-hour reprieve on such grounds.

Rufus was fascinated to learn that great attention was paid to detail, and tender mercy shown in the fine art of hanging. He was struck by the general obsession with mercy. The trial judge himself had prayed for mercy on his soul – a consideration he had found grotesquely incongruous in the solemn pronouncement of the sentence of death: 'Rufus Linton, the sentence of the Court upon you is that you be taken from this place to a lawful prison and thence to a place of execution, and that you there suffer death by hanging. And may the Lord have mercy upon your soul!' Why this misplaced concern for his soul? Why should the judge care, why should anyone care about his soul? Why should anyone show mercy in executing him? The purpose of hanging, he understood, was not to cause suffocation, but rather to dislocate the vertebrae so as to cause a death that was both instantaneous and painless; if the job was to be done properly, the principles of physics had to be applied, with precise calculations being made on the basis of the prisoner's height and weight. Rufus could not help wondering whether all hangmen were conscientious practitioners.

This, then, was the lawful place to which the judge had ordered him to be taken. Countless times before, Rufus had walked by the impregnable-looking structure that announced itself unabashedly as 'The Royal Gaol'. Extending over an entire block in the city of Port-of-Spain, it was itself, at least as it appeared from the outside, a walled city, defensible against siege. Only the moat was lacking. Rufus was convinced that it was all stone and reinforced concrete – built to withstand battering-rams, cannonballs and all manner of enemy attacks, as well as hurricanes in all their fury, to say nothing of attempted escapes. In a manner of speaking, he had been behind bars before, at the Hayes Street side of the College – wrought-iron bars made by D. Rowell & Co. of London SW – stretching and waving his hand with the money, praying that the aloo-pie vendor would get to him next, before recess was over. The bars in his new home were of similarly indestructible construction.

Behind these bars, the prevailing sentiment at the beginning was one of disorientation, caused by his inability to see the mountains of the Northern Range and thus find north. While he soon figured out which way was north, from the time of day and the shadows in the exercise yard, he had lost his tried and trusted compass. He was troubled by the fact that he could seldom practise guessing at the time of day from the position of the sun, since his exposure to the sun was limited. But the loss of his compass troubled him more. It troubled him more than the stench of the hard, made-in-prison, coconut-fibre mattress on which he could see that generations of condemned men had slept before him. It troubled him far, far more than the insufficient ventilation, sunlight and exercise; his feeling of confinement; his longing for mental stimulation; and his blind proximity to the bustle of Frederick Street and the downtown area.

He smiled. He had started thinking about the renowned boys' secondary school on Frederick Street – barely minutes from his current residence in the Royal Gaol – and about the rivalry that had been nurtured for years between that school and the one he had attended. Back at Rufus's College, the derisive comments about the rival used to be on a well-worn theme:

'Give a simple assignment to their brightest student,' one of his teachers or schoolmates would say, 'and you will see how he will sweat over it. He might get it done eventually, but he will make it look hard. He might even pretend it was more complex than it really was, in order to impress. Now give that same simple assignment to anyone at this College and you will see the difference. No sweat. They'll just take it in stride and make it look easy.'

Or someone else might say:

'There is only one College in Port-of-Spain, and it is right here. They shouldn't call that place a College. They should call that place a place.'

No doubt they were equally supercilious at the other place.

Based on a healthy mutual respect, the rivalry, good-natured though it was, could be deadly serious when the schools took each other on at football or in the scholarship stakes. Could it be, Rufus wondered with a wry smile, that the rivalry had got out of control and become truly deadly? Had they been trying to outshine each other in another area of notoriety by vying for the title of most outstanding secondary school in the murder division? Amid all the publicity surrounding the recent hanging of Abdul Malik, there had been reminders that he had spent two years at the other place; Rufus, just sentenced to hang, had attended the College. The score, then, was even.

Where was it he had once read that the prospect of being hanged served to concentrate the mind? He couldn't remember. But he knew it was true, for he found it exceedingly difficult to focus on anything not related to his own mortality. When, as a young child, he had first become conscious of death, he had been terrified. Auntie Mavis had taken him to the funeral of a little girl. Until that day, Rufus hadn't realized that death was irreversible, or that children could die. He demanded answers from Auntie Mavis to scores of questions: 'Can she hear what people are saying?'; 'Is she going to get better and wake up?'; 'Can't she move any part of her body?'; 'Is she going to stay in that box?'; 'Are they going to put me down in a deep hole, too?'; 'Is she going to where she was before she was born?'; 'Where was I

143

before I was born?' For several weeks afterwards, he had nightmares, dreaming that he couldn't move, that he was in a coffin, that he was being buried. It had taken him years to come to terms with the inevitability of death and to stop thinking of what was fair or unfair about it.

In his present situation as one sentenced to death, he initially saw himself as an unlucky, even tragic, figure. He used to indulge himself in thoughts about the various things that his premature death would deny him a chance to do, without bothering to rank them according to their relative importance in the overall scheme of unfulfilment. In his twenty-odd years, he had not left the shores of Trinidad and Tobago. He would never visit one of those countries where people could actually see other people's breath. He would never see snow. He would never disprove for himself what his cousin Pearl had told him – oh, so many years ago! – about those hapless children in northern climes who lost their ears in winter: if they were foolhardy enough to be out playing in the snow and the snow stuck to their ears and they made the mistake of brushing the snow off, the ears came off too. He would never be able to verify Zala's allegation that rats and cockroaches had overrun Brooklyn, New York. He would never have a chance to apply for, let alone take up, the job at the World Bank or the United Nations, that post as economist which well-wishers had once seen in his future. He had a perverse urge to blame those self-same well-wishers for the concatenation of events that had brought him to the death cell. It was because they had inspired him to improve himself and do something with his life that he had messed up his life. If they hadn't put such ideas into his head, he might never have considered going abroad to study, wouldn't have needed a passport, might not have searched so hard for his identity, et cetera, et cetera.

So he would be cut down long before his prime. While he might never have accomplished great things, at least he could have done a few of the mundane things that offer some measure of satisfaction, like finding a decent job (even if it wasn't at a major international organization), having his own place to live, getting married, starting a family. Some of his former classmates were at university; some had been working for several years. He had performed well at school. If things had turned out differently, he might have been engaged in a profession in a couple of years. He pondered these points for quite some time. Then he thought of his friend Rolo, who had died at the age of 16, crushed by a lorry on his way home from school.

That funeral had caused quite a sensation. Entering the church, side by side with the dead boy's parents and brother, two women draped in black were sobbing uncontrollably. Rufus was immediately struck by their sophisticated, majestic and almost imperious air. They were wearing a lot of make-up, and the heavy mascara emphasized the puffy bags under their eyes, which were made to appear unnaturally deep-set. Their drawn, gaunt faces convinced Rufus that they had spent the last couple of days crying and not sleeping. But they still looked attractive. To him, they were like models gracing the cover of a glossy magazine. Large black shawls formed oval frames around their faces, neatly covering their hair and shoulders. Their black dresses must have been sewn by the best seamstress on the island, and their expensive-looking black leather shoes seemed brand new. Obviously, they were sisters. To the untrained eye, they might even have passed for twin sisters, and indeed it was hard to tell them apart or say with certainty which one was younger. But Rufus had an instinctive feeling that the one who looked younger to him was actually older by a couple of years. Be that as it may, he was positive that they were both in their mid-twenties – at least seven years older than Rolo.

On leaving the church, the sisters took up their position next to Rolo's parents and brother, directly behind the hearse, and continued sobbing. The closer the mourners got to the cemetery, the more difficulty Rufus had in containing his perplexity and curiosity. Knowing that Rolo had no sisters, he sought to find out if there was a family relationship, and, if not, what kind of relationship there was between the women and Rolo. Even the most knowledgeable of his classmates could shed no light on the identity of the sobbing sisters, but a woman in the cortège who had overheard the whispers was able to confirm that the women were not related to Rolo by blood or by marriage.

'They live next door,' she volunteered.

The cortège wended its way through the narrow lanes of the cemetery, past ornate, well-tended mausoleums that dwarfed the burial mounds of the forgotten, overgrown with weeds. Rufus noticed, here and there, some wilted flowers and burnt-out candles; it was a few days after All Souls' Day. Then he spotted a huge pile of dirt, and the grave-diggers leaning against a tree. The grave they had dug seemed unusually shallow, somewhat less than six feet, Rufus mused. The rough, uneven walls of the grave gave a vertical section of layers of red clay, reddish dirt and black clayey soil, and made Rufus think of a geological map he had drawn recently to illustrate the stratification of limestone, shale, and sedimentary and igneous rocks.

Rufus positioned himself to have a good view. The mourners gathered round the priest in solemn silence. It was when the coffin was being lowered into the grave that the sisters resumed their sobbing, then intoned a call-and-response lament that soon had tears streaming from Rufus's eyes.

'No, God, don't take him now!' one sister wailed.

'Why you have to go, Rolo?' pleaded the other.

'Take me instead, Lord!'

'O God, Rolo don't leave me! Don't leave me, Rolo!'

Rufus looked around to see who else was crying. The principal of the school, a man who had always appeared so stern and impassive, was sniffing hard and often. Rolo's parents and brother were crying, the father moaning softly. The sisters' plaintive chorus continued, and soon it seemed to Rufus that everyone was desperately fighting back the tears, if not crying openly.

It was the sudden commotion that made Rufus look in the direction of the sisters again. He was exceedingly cross with himself: he should never have taken his gaze off the sisters. He was just in time to see the grave-diggers pulling one of them out of the grave. For several weeks after the funeral, much of the discussion among Rufus's friends had centred on how exactly she had got there. A few said that she had been pushed in by her sister, some said that she had fallen, the majority insisted that she had thrown herself on to the coffin. How Rufus regretted his moment of inattention! At any rate, after she had been pulled out, one of the grave-diggers reached into the excavation to retrieve a shoe she had left behind. No sooner had he handed her the shoe than he hurriedly started shovelling the dirt into the grave, as if not wanting to waste any more time. The thud of dirt and pebbles striking the coffin again reduced all the mourners to solemn silence. Even the sisters no longer sobbed or wailed. They looked dazed by the last dazzling rays of the setting sun, which highlighted the blotches of make-up on their faces and the reddish dirt on the expensive dress of the one who had been in the grave. She looked particularly forlorn with the shoe in her hand.

Soon the coffin was no longer visible. In a matter of minutes, the hole was filled in by the grave-diggers, who continued shovelling until they formed a mound where the hole had been. A woman began placing wreaths on the mound, and then the still air was pierced by a heart-rending scream uttered by Rolo's mother. It sent a chill through Rufus's body, and was like a signal for the mourners to disperse. Rufus walked with two of his friends to the main road, where they took leave of him and boarded a taxi. He then doubled back to the cemetery and took up a vantage point about 15 yards from the grave-site. It was already getting dark, but he could make out the two sisters still standing there. When they finally left, he decided to follow them at what he considered to be a safe distance, and attempted to summon up the courage to speak to them, but before he could, they got into a car and were driven away. He doubted that they had even noticed him. In any case, he was able to squelch the rumour – started a few days later by a school-yard wag – that the sisters had maintained an all-night vigil by Rolo's grave. His classmates accepted his word that he had seen them leave.

When Rufus thought of Rolo's death at the age of 16, he concluded that he himself wasn't so unfortunate after all. At least he wouldn't be caught unawares, for they would eventually tell him when they were going to hang him. This was a civilized country. His head wasn't going to be chopped off with an axe in Woodford Square, at a moment's notice; he would be given a decent hanging in private, behind the walls of the Royal Gaol. Of that, he could rest assured. When the date was set for the hanging, he would be told, as would the rest of the country, so that people like Mano and the roving protester could arrange to be outside the Royal Gaol on execution morning – always on Tuesday, just like market morning was always on Saturday. He would find out on a Thursday evening. The Prison Commissioner would read the death warrant to him, informing him that he was to be hanged the following Tuesday morning. He would be taken to a cell next to the gallows. True, he would have less than a week's notice, but that would give him more than enough time to prepare, to do penance, to repent. He would have the whole weekend to put his soul in order.

He remembered the first time he had been to confession. The aspiring first-communicants, well rehearsed in their Act of Contrition, all looked appropriately contrite. They had been lined up in alphabetical order in the central aisle, and were alternating between two stalls, one on the left, the other on the right of the church. Although Rufus's nerves had him in agony, he was helped by the luck of the alphabet. Having a surname starting with L, and being near the end of the queue, he had time to compose himself. He should have been relieved to note that most of those emerging from the confessionals looked none the worse for wear. But one of the two confessors was rumoured to be a tyrant prone to mete out five rosaries as penance for the most venial of sins, and there was no way of predicting, from the demeanour of the penitents, which box the tyrant was ensconced in. Rufus therefore experienced a fresh surge of nervousness akin to stage fright as he entered the confessional to the right and the priest pulled the slide.

'Bless me, Father, for I have sinned. Father, this is my first confession.'

Already, he was out of breath.

During the weeks of preparation, it had been drummed into the children that they should thoroughly examine their consciences beforehand and be ready to say, without undue pausing or delay, how many times they had committed their sins. Not wanting to be faulted on that score, Rufus rattled off his transgressions:

'I disobeyed my aunt 26 times; I took farina 9 times; I took grapes 7 times; I took apples 4 times; I put a dead mouse on my cousin's bed once; I got into 6 fights at school; and I beat up the girl next door twice; I chewed gum in church once …

For these and all the sins of my past life, especially those I cannot now remember, I humbly ask pardon of God, and penance and absolution of you, Father.'

As instructed, Rufus listened attentively and humbly to the confessor, carefully noting the penance imposed. He felt he had got off lightly with two 'Our Fathers' and five 'Hail Marys', and concluded that the invisible figure absolving him was not the dreaded tyrant.

For many years, he was fortunate not to encounter any confessor deserving of such a qualification, and while the particulars of the recital of transgressions varied, the degree of seriousness remained virtually unchanged. His first experience with a dreaded tyrant came much later and coincided with a confusing period in his life. At the age of 13, he started to have unusual thoughts, feel unusual sensations and take an unusual interest in the female body. It seemed, too, that almost over-night, most of his friends had developed an obsession with matters of sex. Hardly a day passed without some joke, anec-dote or discussion of a sexual nature. Whereas Rufus was still groping with his own innocent ignorance, everyone else seemed amazingly enlightened, Pinhead and Rolo emerging as the leading authorities, ever worldly-wise and not the least bit condescending. It was from the lips of Pinhead that Rufus first heard the term 'erogenous zones', and he was able to research the subject in a manual which Pinhead was generous enough to circulate. Around the same time, Rolo started bringing in magazines with photographs of people of all ages in all their naked glory. With a mixture of shame and fascination, Rufus studied the pictures, as well as the articles extolling the virtues of nudism.

It didn't take Rufus long to form the conclusion that his unusual thoughts were impure and needed to be confessed. He decided to go, but was filled with almost as much apprehension as when he had made his first confession. This time, his worst fears were realized; he found the priest severe, irascible and intent on knowing everything. Rufus tried to put most of the blame on Rolo and Pinhead, for each time he listened to their instructive assertions or consulted their visual materials, he was invariably assailed by a fresh onset of impure thoughts. But when the disembodied voice asked him pointedly if he ever had such thoughts when he was alone and not reading books or looking at pictures, Rufus told the truth. As penance, he had to say the rosary three times. How Rolo laughed when Rufus told him about it!

He was left to wonder how many rosaries Rolo would have been directed to say, if he had ever had to go to confession. His own impure thoughts were innocent nothings compared to the exploits Rolo used to boast of. He was persuaded by the lamentation of the two sisters at Rolo's funeral that those boasts had not been idle. On the other hand, he, Rufus Linton, without placing any premium on his virginity, was stuck with it for life and was going to die a virgin, in common with the millions who died before that question even arose for them, and in common with the countless others who chose, for religious or other reasons, to preserve their virginity for life. Was the prison chaplain in that category?

'Do popes have to be virgins?' Rufus asked the chaplain.

'They are celibate.'

'So they don't have to be virgins?'

'I don't think it's a requirement before they begin a life of celibacy,' ventured the chaplain.

'What about nuns?'

'They have to be chaste.'

'But do they have to be virgins?' Rufus persisted.

'I am a virgin,' he volunteered after a pause, looking expectantly at the chaplain. The latter maintained the inscrutable physiognomy of one accustomed to hearing confidences without revealing any of his own, a face that said: 'Don't ask me about myself.'

Is chastity a state of mind? Am I chaste? Rufus wondered to himself later. Are my fantasies as sinful as the real thing? Do my impure thoughts make me less than chaste even though I'm a virgin? He should have asked the chaplain those questions, as well as questions about the chaplain's own virginity. But would any answers have been given? It wasn't the first time he had spoken to the Catholic priest assigned to the prison. Early on, the latter had taken the initiative in attempting to proffer spiritual guidance and comfort, but had been rebuffed. In the fullness of time, however, feeling ready to initiate a discussion, Rufus had asked to see him. Nor was it the first time the chaplain had failed to assuage his appetite for answers. Strangely, though, priestly evasiveness was growing on Rufus. Whereas he used to be irritated by the half-smiles, he found himself beginning to like the chaplain's way of not saying too much, not giving anything away.

His intuition assured him that the chaplain was not a virgin. One couldn't tell just by looking at him, but hadn't he had a clear chance to say that he was a virgin, and hadn't he declined to say so? Rufus's willing and impassive embrace of that conclusion differed strikingly from his incredulity years earlier when a history teacher had matter-of-factly told the class about a pope who had fathered children.

Having made no pledge of celibacy, Rufus was unlikely to come to terms with that enforced state. It was definitely not by choice that he was going to die a virgin, and the matter of his incomplete courtship loomed more vexing than before. Maybe the outcome would have been different if Dr Inspector had died intestate.

He had been wrong again – wrong to think he would ever overcome the disappointment of not seeing Sally at his trial. Now he tried to rationalize the fact that since his imprisonment, she had not once honoured him with a note, much less a visit. His lawyer Nozick had come a few times to discuss an appeal, but Auntie Mavis was the only person who continued to visit regularly. Why should Sally act differently from his colleagues at the College, his friends and his own relatives? She owed him nothing, after all. She had never promised anything, had never said she loved him, had never, for that matter, given any indication, tangible or otherwise, that she loved him. So what logic was there in feeling so let down? Such a sharp sense of betrayal and disappointment was certainly uncalled for. Nevertheless, how good it would have been to have a visit from Sally as one of his final earthly pleasures, to see her at least once before he died!

Maybe that should be his last wish. It was said that many of those who had gone to the gallows before him had requested pig-food souse, shrimp roti, hops and shark, or some other delicacy for their last meal. Maybe he could keep his request simple, a last meal of bread and water, and petition for a visit from Sally in lieu of fancy food – and why not an intimate encounter, so that at least once before he died, he could be as unchaste in deed as in mind and make reality correspond to fantasy? But surely there were limits to what the authorities would agree to as his last wish. In any case, it was futile to fantasize. Yet the sheer futility of the fantasy failed to lessen its appeal or impede the full play of his imagination. Sally might have forgotten his very existence, but he could possess her in his imagination.

He should have been grateful to the chaplain and forgiven him for being so laconic and enigmatic. Wasn't he owed a debt of gratitude for helping Rufus towards new insights: that celibacy was not necessarily synonymous with virginity; that Rufus's enforced state of celibacy was not necessarily a state of grace? In a series of imaginary conversations, Rufus found himself engaging in elaborate sophistry, while ever on the lookout for loopholes and inconsistencies on the part of the chaplain. In the actual conversations, he would have been more than satisfied just to get answers.

'I did something really terrible,' Rufus said to the chaplain. 'I killed my own mother. But I might even go to Heaven. All I have to do is die in a state of grace.'

He wondered how he would know if he was in a state of grace, and the chaplain looked at him as if he could hear him wondering. He prayed that he wouldn't be asked if he felt true remorse.

He told the chaplain he didn't think it was fair; average conduct over a lifetime ought to figure in the evaluation of qualifications for admission to Heaven. A man kills his mother, repents before being hanged, and goes to Heaven. A good man dies suddenly, before he can repent of some solitary mortal sin, and goes to hell. The chaplain told him it was probably not so straightforward.

'Sin is sin, and dead is dead, and hell is hell,' said Rufus.

The chaplain told him that there were mysteries that could not be explained, questions that could not be answered in this life.

Many years earlier, it was Rufus's cousin Pearl who had first complained to Auntie Mavis about his penchant for raising awkward questions and causing embarrassment. Rufus was six at the time, and Auntie Mavis had decided that he should start going to church. She thought it would be heartless to wake him up to go to the 5 a.m. mass with her, so Pearl, as the eldest of the three cousins in the house, was commissioned to take him. Rufus was thrilled: he was sporting a smart haircut and the brand-new outfit bought by Auntie Mavis.

To Rufus, there was neither rhyme nor reason to what was happening in the church. He didn't understand the language being spoken. Everybody was standing up, then sitting down, then kneeling down, then sitting down, then standing up. At times, some people sang, while others mumbled; at times, some people mumbled, while others were silent. And there were strange smells, and something like smoke. Then at one point, when everybody else was sitting down, two men started going from row to row with red bags attached to long poles. As each man pushed his bag in front of the people, some of them appeared to put money in it, but others did not see it.

'What are they doing?' Rufus asked Pearl.

'Taking up the collection.'

'What is that?' he asked.

'They are collecting money.'

'Who is it for?' he persisted.

Pearl was more and more embarrassed, especially as Rufus was speaking at the top of his voice.

'I'll explain later,' she whispered.

Soon one of the men reached Rufus's row. Pearl dropped something in the bag, and just as it was about to go past Rufus, he asked Pearl, again at the top of his voice:

'Can I have 25 cents please?'

The bag remained suspended under his nose, while Pearl fumbled for a 25-cent piece. Moments later, the bag was still suspended, as Rufus closely examined the coin. The bag was jerked away when Rufus put the coin in his pocket, appearing not to see the man holding the pole. But Pearl did notice the man, and was to report to Auntie Mavis that he gnashed his teeth in disgust.

During the Eucharist, Rufus was afraid to be left behind, and loudly insisted that he should accompany Pearl up to the communion-rail. In the end, she decided not to go.

Then the two men came back with their red bags attached to poles. Rufus was intrigued:

'What do they want now?'

Pearl ignored the question and, like so many others, did not see the red bag, which was much lighter than the first time round. Rufus brought it to her attention:

'How come you didn't put anything in?'

Pearl never took Rufus to church again. He continued to raise awkward questions, often confounding his catechism teachers. Some thought he was simply being perverse; others thought he had a genuine desire to know.

There was no way of telling what the prison chaplain thought. He wasn't very forthcoming, and did far more listening than talking. So most of Rufus's questions were unresolved and were likely to remain so.

On the inside cover of the Bible Rufus had borrowed from Auntie Mavis, there was an inscription reading: 'To Mary Alexandra on the occasion of her Christening from Uncle Jeremy & Auntie Lynne. 28th Feb 1954'. As a school assignment, he had once had to write the autobiography of a shoe, and he now toyed with the idea of recounting the peregrination of his copy of the Bible: 'From a Christening to a Murderer's Cell'. He felt there had to be some fascinating story behind it. He wondered who Mary Alexandra was. He wondered what route the Bible had taken from her to the second-hand bookseller from whom

Auntie Mavis had bought it. Second-hand though it was, it remained in pristine condition. No doubt Mary Alexandra, whoever she was, had not had much use for it.

But Rufus did. He had taken to browsing through it in order to while away the time. It was in the course of such browsing that, to his surprise, he discovered his name in Mark's narrative of the Passion: 'And they compel one Simon a Cyrenian, who passed by, coming out of the country, the father of Alexander and Rufus, to bear his cross.' He shouldn't have been surprised; he had heard of parents opening the Bible at random and giving their child whatever name their eyes fell upon – unless it happened to be something like Cain or Jezebel or Judas. Still, his interest was piqued, and with the excitement of being on the verge of an unusual find, he began searching for further references to his Biblical namesake. He discovered that both Luke and Matthew mentioned Simon without mentioning Rufus, but it was a mystery why John mentioned neither Simon nor Rufus.

Was Rufus, son of Simon, just a footnote? Rufus Linton remained intrigued. He raised the question with the chaplain, who admitted he couldn't see the point of it all, but promised to do some research. He brought back word that Rufus should read the Epistle of Paul the Apostle to the Romans: 'Salute Rufus chosen in the Lord, and his mother and mine.' The discomfort which the reference to mother caused Rufus was quelled by another question he had for the chaplain: was the Rufus who was chosen in the Lord the selfsame son of Simon? The chaplain hedged.

In the end, Rufus could only bow to the conclusion that the chaplain was right: it was pointless. 'Rufus' wasn't even his real name. To find his true namesake, he would have to look for 'Prince', and there must be hundreds of princes mentioned in the Bible.

Apparently taking Rufus's interest in the Bible as an indication that further spiritual support would be welcome, the chaplain broached the possibility of a visit from the Legion of Mary. Once a week, two senior members of the Legion came to the Royal Gaol. Always operating in consultation with the chaplain, they were happy to follow his suggestions about inmates they might talk to. Rufus was enthusiastic; he remembered the respect and admiration he had felt for his cousin Pearl, a dedicated Legionary at one time. He tried to remember if prisoners were on her rounds. He knew that in addition to visiting children at orphanages, she used to assist the homebound and the bedridden, but he couldn't remember her ever talking about going to a prison.

'I already know what the Legion does,' said Rufus, interrupting the Legionary just as she had started to explain. Interrupting her was a feat requiring superb timing – she talked so fast she took his breath away.

'My name is Josephine and her name is Erica,' she had rattled off, as if Erica had been incapable of speaking for herself or unwilling to introduce herself. And without excessive preliminaries, she had asked Rufus:

'Would you like us to say the rosary?'

'I don't have a chaplet,' he objected.

'Erica will let you have her beads,' Josephine volunteered, and Erica obligingly surrendered them through the intervention of a prison officer in the visiting area.

The prayers were led by Josephine, and Rufus had time to think about how thin she was. It must have been because she burned up calories just by talking, he mused. Then the word 'zwill' came into his head and took him back to his kite-flying days. It was a ruthless business, competitive kite-flying. Attached to the tails of the combatant kites, broken razor blades

– zwill – played a strategic and offensive role as the kite-flyer hauled his string this way and that, brusquely jerked it down a bit or played on it with deftness and finesse, trying to manoeuvre the kite for an attacking dive to cut down another kite, or hoping to coax it into a safe area where it might evade enemy zwill.

'Zwill'. In connection with a kite as it sailed aloft in the whistling wind, its tail lethally fitted with broken razor blades, the word had wonderful euphony. But there was no kind or charitable way to call a person 'zwill'. In reference to Josephine, it couldn't be taken for a term of endearment, since it meant that she was thinner than a rake. Indeed she was. She reminded Rufus of the roving protester at the Red House. She was just as thin and almost as angular, but she carried her thinness with greater grace and self-assurance, and through her chirpy disposition, merry eyes and melodious voice, she exuded an altogether different aura. For all her thinness, there was nothing frail about her, only a wholesome vitality that made her glow with health all over.

Her narrow waist was girded by a wide, brightly coloured plastic belt that Rufus found too cheap and gaudy, considering the overall demure effect of her long-sleeved, full-length dress of sober colour. Erica was wearing a plain, short-sleeved cotton blouse, tucked into a skirt – also of decorous length – with a chequered pattern of green and blue. Rufus continued studying them after they had finished the rosary and during the ensuing conversation, again dominated by Josephine. As he studied them, he tried to imagine how they would have looked in veils and wimples back in the days when all nuns were so attired. And as he was creating that mental picture, the question popped out of his mouth:

'Are you going to become nuns?'

For once, Josephine spoke slowly: 'I don't think so.' Erica shook her head, but Rufus said to himself that if one of the two was to become a nun, it would surely be Erica.

'Keep the chaplet,' Josephine said as they were leaving.

Long after they had gone, he was still vacillating, still unsure whether he found them good-looking, whether he was attracted to them in the same way he was attracted to Sally. He knew he enjoyed the vibrations he felt in their company. To him, they made a perfectly coordinated pair; he doubted that they ever squabbled. They complemented each other, one doing most of the talking, the other mainly listening.

He realized, though, that he had paid relatively little attention to Erica. That must have been the pattern whenever she was with the dominant Josephine, the one everybody noticed first. He wondered how Erica felt about living in Josephine's shadow and contributing just the amens. Wasn't there bound to be at least a trace of resentment? Was she genuinely resigned to her fate? Was she less content to play second fiddle than she appeared to be? He promised himself to pay more attention to her the next time.

Rufus's pulse quickened when they greeted him with full-face smiles the next time. Already Erica's fingers were delicately rolling the beads of a chaplet that replaced the one she had given him. (How many did she own?) The last time, he had failed to notice how disproportionately long her fingers were, and to pick up the smell of cigarettes from her clothing. As on the first visit, both pairs of knees were demurely covered, Josephine's by a full skirt, Erica's by a dress gaily embroidered around the neck and bottom hem – obviously home-made by a mediocre seamstress. Erica, he reckoned, was about five foot eight inches, marginally taller, yet not much stouter than Josephine. He detected some ungainliness in her deportment; her shoulders were bowed forward slightly as if she were afraid to stand to her full height.

Her forehead was prominent, both because of the way she combed her hair and because she hardly had any eyebrows. She overcompensated for that scarcity with a luxuriant head of unruly hair, which she twirled with her spare hand at random intervals. From the slant of her eyes – piercing eyes that carried conviction – and from the contours of their inner margins and outer corners, he was positive that there was Chinese in her ancestry. Her whole demeanour conveyed serenity, amiability and tolerance.

After they had said the rosary, Rufus asked, feeling like Sherlock Holmes: 'How come you smoke, Erica?'

'I just can't stop,' she replied, nodding, smiling, playing with her hair and making Rufus retreat from his earlier certainty that she was destined for a life of chastity, obedience and poverty. She was a mystery which he would never unravel. He was more confused than ever. What motivated these 20-year-olds to spend their spare time on good works? Did they like Carnival, dancing, going to the pictures? Was this the beginning of a lifetime of devoutness or just a phase? The questions he wanted to ask were many and he didn't know which one to put first. He was later to take himself to task for making a most unfortunate choice: 'Do you know about the children of Mary?'

'I never heard about it,' Josephine said. 'Is it a branch of the Legion?'

Rufus hastened to clarify: 'No, that's not what I mean. I mean the other children Mary had, after Jesus.'

Bewilderment was painted on the Legionaries' faces.

'Did you ever read what Mark says about Jesus teaching in the synagogue?' Rufus inquired. 'He says that many of the listeners were astonished and started asking: "Is not this the carpenter, the son of Mary, the brother of James, and Joses, and of Juda, and Simon? and are not his sisters here with us?"'

'Where in the Bible does it say that?' demanded Josephine, incredulous.

'In Mark, he said,' Erica contributed.

'Do you know the Bible by heart?' Josephine asked, directing the question at Rufus and ignoring Erica.

'Not yet,' he replied.

Erica twirled her hair and made no further effort to participate in the discussion. Rufus suddenly felt irritated by that tic-like habit of hers, and the Legionaries probably both sensed his irritation. Erica followed Josephine's cue in getting ready to leave, even as Rufus continued:

'Do you read the Bible? Have you ever read the Bible? Let us read the Bible next time. You should find out about Mary's children, if you are the Legion of Mary.'

Immediately he said it, he realized it had all come out wrong, and he wished he could have taken it back. He would explain, next time. He would make amends. He would not be lax, next time. He would be ready to say the rosary when they came. He would already have the chaplet in his hand, next time.

There was no next time. They must have found some other prisoner to say the rosary with. Rufus was positive that they had reported the discussion to the chaplain and that he had told them not to return. He was just as powerless to prove it as he had been to prove that Mr Scobie had poisoned his dog Twinkle. But no other explanation came forward.

Rufus turned his attention away from the Bible and started reading other material as a way of taking his mind off questions of the after-life. He had once been a voracious reader. At school, his classmates had joked that he carried around a piece of plastic in his pocket, so that he could read in the rain without getting his book all wet. For some time after that cruel, baseless rumour had reached his ears, Rufus had taken great pains to avoid being seen reading by his persecutors, but his appetite remained unsatisfied. Even Auntie Mavis used to warn him that he was reading too much for his own good.

'You're going to spoil your eyes, boy. And then you will have to wear glasses. You want them to call you a four-eyed bookworm?'

But that had been a good while ago. Since leaving school, he had had little time for books, other than those with which he was supposed to be familiar in his role as teacher. There had been too much else to do. Now there would be a little time. The question was where to begin. Which books deserved the distinction of being counted among the last to be read by Rufus Linton? They would have to be acknowledged masterpieces. The little time that was left was not to be wasted on trash. So he picked up the *Complete Works of Shakespeare*, and it opened on a bookmark formed by five folded pages filled with the neat handwriting he used to have. It was his essay on "Life in the New World before the Coming of Columbus", the imposition that had never been collected by his history teacher in the first form. After rereading it with suitable self-admiration, he plunged into *Macbeth*, undaunted by the prospect of the *Complete Works* from cover to cover.

It was like being back in the fifth form. Only this time he wasn't required to memorize long passages or think of context questions. He didn't even stop to puzzle over strange turns of phrase. But he did stop, just before the first murder, in order to analyse himself. Why had he started reading a play which he knew was about murder? Murder most foul. Murder planned, premeditated, with malice aforethought. He hated murder. Macbeth, get thee hence! And take Boysie Singh and Boland Ramkissoon with thee!

What had made him think about Boysie Singh? It was not inconceivable that Boysie might have slept in the same bed, in the same condemned cell that Rufus now occupied. But Boysie Singh and Rufus Linton! Wasn't it incongruous to mention their names in the same breath? A book had been written about Boysie, who had become a legend long before he was hanged. He had joined the panoply of real or imagined bugaboos invoked by children at play. Word that the Green-Faced Man, Tall Boy or Boysie Singh was coming was enough to provoke squeals and giggles of a terror that was almost real. Rufus and his friends used to catch lizards and dissect them. One day they decided on a novel form of execution for a hapless pair: they tied string round their necks and hanged them from the branch of a guava-tree; they dug a little hole under the tree; they placed the bodies of the lizards in two matchboxes, which they buried in the hole. The matchboxes were labelled 'Boysie Singh' and 'Boland Ramkissoon'. Rufus thought about those lizards as the story of Boysie Singh crossed his mind. It was said that Boysie and Boland had been assigned adjoining death cells, and that as the fateful Tuesday approached, there had been bitter recriminations between the two – Boland cursing the day he had first met Boysie, whom he accused of leading him to the hangman, and Boysie cursing the day he had first met Boland, the jinx who had caused his luck to run out. But there was no one for Rufus to blame. And the more he thought about it, the more he felt sorry for himself, only to castigate himself a few minutes later for wallowing so shamelessly in self-pity.

He ought to stop complaining. True, he couldn't look forward to any more visits from the Legionaries. True, he couldn't stop thinking how good it would be to see Sally just once. True, he had been disowned by most members of the Linton clan. But at least he could depend on regular visits from

Auntie Mavis. He had much more contact with the outside world than most of the inmates he knew. Rarely did anyone come to see Moby. No one ever came to see Yank.

Moby had been convicted of murdering Leon Laurent, the younger brother of the founder of a well-known confectionery factory. Moby was a compulsive talker and seemed to know everything about the Laurent family. He could recount the most intriguing details of the history of the factory, from the time when old Mr Laurent came down from Haiti with his life savings and lifelong determination to make money, to the time when he was crushed by his own mango-tree. Old Mr Laurent's wife never forgave herself; it had been her idea to have the tree cut down, always announcing to all and sundry that it was responsible for the mould in the bathroom. 'It cuts off the sunlight. The place is too musty,' she used to say. Old Mr Laurent didn't share her opinion on the question of mould, mustiness and the mango-tree; the tree had come with the house and, to him, went very well with the house; they were even essential to and inseparable from each other, the tree keeping the house shaded and cool, however blistering the heat. Yet he had no strong feelings on the matter and was not an argumentative type, though he did, on one occasion, point out to his wife that the mango-tree hadn't done anybody any harm; it would have to be cut down over his dead body. But that had been after a family reunion at which he had succumbed to temptation and sampled some home-made wine – an episode he had talked about the following week at his Alcoholics Anonymous meeting. It was a few days after that momentary aberration that he had resolved to have done with it:

'I will cut the tree down myself.'

Although old Mr Laurent had never even trimmed a hedge, let alone cut a tree down, he was quite handy, and reckoned he could handle the mango-tree. He could have told Moby to do it.

Moby was strong and always willing. While having lunch one day with the owner of a biscuit factory, old Mr Laurent had heard about Moby crawling on a 100-pound block of ice into a furnace, while it was still hot, in order to carry out urgent repairs to the bricks. He had thus prevented any slow-down in production. The account of this exploit had filled old Mr Laurent with such fascination that he confided to his wife:

'I have to find this man Moby and get him to work for us.'

So said, so done. Old Mr Laurent personally sought out Moby, enticed him away from the biscuit factory, and never had cause to regret it. There was nobody in the world who could work as hard as Moby. And if at 3 o'clock on a Sunday morning, old Mr Laurent sent word that Moby was needed, the latter would rush out of his house and come at once.

'Get Moby to cut down the tree,' Mrs Laurent advised.

'His son is getting married in Cedros. He asked me about it a long time ago. I told him it was all right. That he could go.'

'Well, wait till he comes back,' Mrs Laurent said.

Old Mr Laurent, thinking that the discussion had gone on long enough, simply stated:

'Tomorrow is Sunday. I don't have too much to do. I will cut down the mango-tree for you.'

Seconds after the chicken began sizzling in the pot, Mrs Laurent's blood curdled at the crashing sound of falling timber and her husband's piercing cry for help. By the time they managed to move the tree off his unconscious body, he had already lost too much blood. Although he lingered on for half a day, no one expected a miracle.

Moby bawled more than he had bawled at his own father's funeral, and blamed himself for the tragedy: he should have been there when he was needed.

The younger of the Laurent brothers had never been an amiable person. He had never taken any great interest in the business, and agreed only with undisguised reluctance to take over the factory when his brother died. Almost overnight the factory began to lose money for the first time in its history. Leon surrounded himself with incompetent cronies, who invariably gave him bad advice. They launched a new line of gumdrops called 'Laurencines'; it flopped after a four-year-old choked to death on one, and after a scandal sheet alleged that the factory was operating under unhygienic conditions.

Before too long, the ill-fated house was put up for sale. Mrs Laurent was not unhappy to leave. The bathroom remained as musty and mouldy as ever, and the stump of the mango-tree was a daily reminder of the tragedy. She tried to have the stump removed, but was told that that might damage the foundations of the house. Leon Laurent and his advisers took charge of the sale, and when it was completed, gave Mrs Laurent a small percentage of the proceeds. The remainder, they told her, had to be ploughed back into the factory to keep it afloat.

Mrs Laurent didn't complain, but Moby felt she was being treated unfairly. He felt even more aggrieved on her behalf when he discovered that the factory had reduced her pension and had become erratic in making the payments. He talked with some of the other workers about this, and the consensus was that whatever the current misfortunes of the business, the widow of the man who had put his whole life into the factory should be guaranteed a decent living. They agreed that Moby, the trusty dogsbody of old Mr Laurent, should raise the issue with the new management.

Leon Laurent (who by now had acquired the nickname 'Fireman', because he was constantly firing people, often for no good reason) was outraged at the effrontery of this mere labourer.

Leon threatened to fire Moby on the spot unless he left his presence and got back to work immediately. Moby stood his ground. In the ensuing argument, Moby told Leon that he and his friends should stop squandering the factory's money on women. Moby, a man of immense bulk and brawn, was staggered by the blow which Leon delivered to his face. In an instant, he recovered, but Leon was already running for his life.

They must have run for at least a mile and a half, Leon shouting 'Murder!' and 'Help!', Moby just heaving hard. The people they sped past knew intuitively that this was a life-and-death struggle. A couple of energetic loiterers started running behind them, more out of ghoulish interest in the climax than out of any illusion that they could alter the outcome. Leon and Moby ran through the front gates of a school, across the deserted quadrangle, and through a crowded classroom. In quick succession, they jumped through a window at the back of the room, and on to a playground a few feet below. When Leon stumbled, Moby grabbed his shirt, but was unable to prevent him from darting off again, in the direction of the back gate. Five minutes earlier, the gate would have been open for the last of the latecomers.

Leon wasn't quick enough in clambering up the iron gate. Moby dragged him down. According to the medical report, he stabbed Leon fifty-two times.

For the next week, there were few competing subjects of discussion. Moby had just kept on running. His picture was in the newspapers, and people were checking and double-checking their doors. It was on a thickly wooded hillside near Maracas Beach that the police found him asleep one afternoon.

Moby told the court that the blood had rushed up to his head. He also protested that the police had beaten him up, even though he had offered no resistance. But the trial didn't last long.

Virtually everything Rufus knew about Yank he had gleaned from Moby. In the absence of corroboration or rebuttal on the part of Yank, he was resigned to taking Moby's word as gospel.

'Yank? What kind of name is that?' Rufus inquired.

'It's not his real name,' Moby explained. 'People call him that because his father is American.'

According to Moby, Yank did not know his father – a serviceman once stationed at the Chaguaramas base – and had grown up in an orphanage. Yank, said Moby, had been found guilty of holding up and killing a truck driver on a beer-delivery run. Also according to Moby, the driver had actually been shot by an accomplice, but the latter had never been apprehended, partly because Yank would not talk. That was the nature of the man: he would not talk. Rufus could think of no one to match Yank in the uncommunicative department.

He could see that eating was a private matter between Yank and his food. Yank rarely lifted his eyes from his plate. He fastidiously kept foods from different groups apart, making sure his meat didn't mingle with his rice. He held the spoon in his left hand, and his sinewy left forearm seemed to curve over and round the plate in a protective formation. His manner of eating was both deliberate and audible: not only did the spoon scrape the plate, but he made up for his withholding of conversation with assorted slurping and gurgling sounds. Rufus could hear him chew, swallow and digest.

He felt sorry for Yank. It was more than empathy. It was unadulterated pity for one whose unrelieved wretchedness he would never come close to enduring. He felt sorrier for Yank than he felt for himself, even with his own bankruptcy of conscience and the ignominious lack of remorse that could not be divulged to anyone.

'You deserve what's coming to you, you matricidal Rufus Linton!' he said to himself.

Matricide, parricide. Words he had discovered in Latin class. Julius Caesar, Gaul, Carthaginian War. *Amo, amas, amat*. Ablatives. Supines. They all came back to him, accompanied by snatches of Latin from his old missal, with the Latin and the English side by side, Latin on the left page, English on the right. *Sed tantum dic verbo … Qui tollis peccata mundi …* He used to know all of that, all the responses, all the prayer endings. And then one day, the Latin stopped. Just as he was learning his first conjugation at school, the Latin stopped in church. In the vernacular, in the language of the people, the mass was foreign, unnatural, and he missed the *Dominus vobiscum*.

Matricide, parricide. He remembered Latin class, and the time when he was sentenced by the Latin master to five consecutive evenings in detention for writing on the blackboard:

Latin is a language
As dead as dead can be
It has killed the Romans
And now it's killing me.

What was the point of it all? To have suffered through so many unseens, so many declensions, so many conjugations, only to end up where the Jamaican fast bowler, Leslie Hylton, had ended up – on the hangman's noose.

Of all the commentaries that might be offered on his condition, the wryest of all came from the title of the masquerade band that had just been adjudged the best of the year – Stephen Lee Heung's 'Paradise Lost', designed by Peter Minshall. Oh yes, he could relate to that. Was Carnival more fun than Christmas? Which one would he sooner give up? As a child he used to say that he preferred both. Now he thought he had part of the answer. It was more severe a punishment to be locked up in the Royal Gaol at Carnival time than at Christmas. Since December, he had been hearing the latest calypsos on the radio. Little Scobie's composition about Boris the asylum-seeker was getting less and less air play and was starting to sound stale in comparison with the more recent tunes. Often at night he could hear in the distance the strains of Lord Kitchener's 'Pan in Harmony' being rehearsed by a steel orchestra, and he would try to guess from which panyard the wind was blowing. He had read about wine connoisseurs doing blind wine-tastings, and he felt a certain kinship with them. By the time the preliminaries for the steelband competition began, he knew by heart the arrangements of the calypsos to be played by three orchestras. When only two of them continued practising during the following week, he knew that the third had been eliminated. One night, one of the surviving orchestras surprised him by experimenting with the arrangement he had grown to love, but after a couple of hours he no longer missed the little pieces they had left out, and loved the little pieces they had put in.

His excitement awoke him long before dawn on Carnival Monday. So distracting was his excitement that he nearly forgot to say 'Rabbit, Rabbit, Rabbit' as a way of guaranteeing himself good fortune for the entire month of March. Three years earlier, he had gone missing between Carnival Sunday night and the early hours of Ash Wednesday, for which he had been subjected to a stern sermon from Auntie Mavis. His comment that he should have been welcomed back like the Prodigal Son had done nothing to appease her; she had seen that as impudence verging on blasphemy. But now he realized that he had been right to abscond for what had turned out to be one of his last bouts of merrymaking as a free man. The experience of the following

Carnival failed to satisfy him. With some money in his pocket from his first few months of teaching, he had set his heart on a fancy sailor costume, but, swayed by Auntie Mavis, had ended up portraying a medieval prince. He was sorry he had let her change his mind. By the time the next Carnival came round, he was in the throes of the search for his mother's identity, and felt in no mood for revelry. He forfeited the deposit on his costume.

From his listening post, Carnival Monday was dull. About half past six in the morning, he heard a superb steelband rendition of *Eine kleine Nachtmusik*, but after that, the faint, intermittent boom of drums in the distance was the only sound to remind him of the significance of the day. After lunch, he counted just two masquerade bands passing by the Royal Gaol.

On Carnival Tuesday, he felt he was being tortured. From round mid-morning until after dark, his cell reverberated. When it wasn't Lord Kitchener's 'Flag Woman', it was Lord Nelson's 'La La'. It seemed as if all the disc jockeys on the trucks, all the brass bands, all the steel orchestras had decided to pause in front of the Royal Gaol and give a command performance. He didn't hear the three steelband arrangements he knew so well, but he was positive he heard the three orchestras in question, playing different numbers. Straining his ears, he thought he could make out the sound of scores of shuffling feet. He could visualize scenes from his childhood: rows of sailors shuffling in formation, left to right, right to left. How he would have loved to masquerade in one of those sailor bands, to do the sailor dance, the rolling dance with the walking stick, to carry a large can of baby powder, to throw powder in the air, to sprinkle it on all and sundry!

Early in the afternoon, he deduced that the congestion of bands lining up to enter the parade grounds at the Savannah was at its worst. A brass band – which sounded very much like

Gemini Brass, but might easily have been Kalyan – performed before the prison gates for over an hour, unable to advance any further up Frederick Street. At one point, he was treated to a jam session. It was in fact a musical tapestry that seemed to have been in the repertoire of every local dance band for generations. It was often reserved for the end of a party, when it never failed to infuse fresh energy into the weary with its familiar phrases and predictable bridges. It started without melody, with only the rhythmic pulse of the percussion section defining a steady beat and setting the tempo for the exposition of eight quarter notes by the bass guitar, each quarter note getting one count, with four counts to a measure. The sequence was repeated three times before the rhythm guitar joined a chord to each bass note to form the unifying pattern of chord progressions. Then came a trumpet call in four measures, presenting the thematic material, stating a theme that harked back to some fanfare of old as revitalized and rejuvenated in a calypso beat. The theme of the fanfare provided the basis for the building of solos, riffs, harmonies, variations and improvisations by the entire brass section, with ever-changing instrumental combinations, saxophone responding to trumpet, trombone responding to saxophone, trumpet responding to trombone. Rufus could picture the trombonists briskly moving the slides back and forth. Towards the end of each cycle, he could hear the trombones produce an elongated, plaintive note and give a fleeting feeling of conclusion, before the theme of the fanfare was restated by the saxophones. And he was awed by the combined vocal power of the revellers adding their own counterpoint over the blast of the trumpets. He hoped he would be hanged long before the next Carnival so that he would never again have to endure the ordeal of being blind.

One night Rufus dreamt that the sentence had been carried out and that his body was being cremated. During the cremation, it seemed as if his spirit were hovering in the sky, observing acquaintances and strangers all over Trinidad and Tobago. He was acutely aware of what people were saying and thinking about him. He could see men going through his belongings in his cell and finding a manuscript of his. Then, amid a swirl of events, he could hear praise being lavished on his work. He had become a famous writer, so famous that people were saying what a shame it was that the life of a young man of such talent had been cut short so brutally. Just before he awoke, with a splitting headache and in total confusion, he had the sensation of being in a coffin.

In his childhood nightmares, he had been trapped in a coffin. But the rest of this new dream was altogether unfamiliar and puzzling. With great ease, he was able to reconstruct bits and pieces, but he had trouble establishing whether it had been a single dream or separate related dreams. He thought that the part about the cremation didn't ring true; as far as he knew, all those who had preceded him to the gallows had been buried, and he himself had never entertained the idea of being cremated. Also, he couldn't understand why he should be in a coffin if he had already been cremated.

For all his perplexity, he was suddenly filled with a sense of mission, a sense of urgency, an awareness of the need to set priorities; he could ill afford to wait for posthumous fame. There and then, he determined not to read any more of the magazines or books given to him by the chaplain and other visitors. He knew he ran no risk of being bored; he would keep his mind active as usual, always busy speculating or wondering about something. He would read the newspaper, but only what he considered to be the hard-news segments, or the sports page, studiously avoiding anything that had to do with fiction or had any resemblance to creative writing.

At first, nobody knew about the resolution he had made to himself. It was several days later, when Auntie Mavis started bringing him murder-mystery novels, that he broke his silence on this point.

'I am never going to read a book again,' he announced.

Astonishment mixed with repentance, as Auntie Mavis blamed herself for being so silly, for being so thoughtless as to give him murder mysteries. How painful it must have been for him to read about poisons, guns and other implements of murder, let alone the graphic accounts of stabbings! But Rufus, who had felt compelled to put *Macbeth* aside, sought to reassure her:

'I would not be affected by what is in those books.'

And he left it at that.

Rufus had concluded that his dream had been a sign. He had only a little time left, and he was not to spend that time reading what others had created; he was to create something himself. And so it was that he set about planning his book. The trouble was that he didn't know what he wanted to write about. His own story? Who would be interested? He didn't consider himself to be that fascinating a murderer, as murderers go. Rufus Linton was no Boysie Singh, he reminded himself. In any event, there were already biographies and autobiographies and ghost-written autobiographies of murderers aplenty. Why not create something different? To do this, he would have to cleanse his mind, or at least try to. Try to cast out the demons. Not allow his book to be infected by the influence of his favourite writers. Or maybe distil the various influences and extract the essence in order to produce a totally new creation.

'Your days are numbered, Linty,' he said to himself. 'You have already read enough, and you simply don't have time to read any more. Make that dream come true.'

It took Rufus far less time to complete what he envisaged as the first section of 'The Story of Drag' than to get permission to have it published. The prison authorities had never received such a request, and didn't know how to proceed. One day Rufus was told that 'Mr B' wanted to see him. The first thing that Rufus noticed about Mr B's office was a large, weather-beaten, wooden desk, which was virtually bare, and the first thing he noticed about Mr B was a toothpick, stuck like a permanent appendage in the left corner of his mouth. On the desk there was an ashtray – the size of a soup-plate – that seemed to have been carved out of a rock. In the ashtray there were at least a dozen chewed-up toothpicks. Next to the ashtray there was the most impressive name-plate Rufus had ever seen, made of mahogany, polished to a gloss, with the name 'RUFUS BRODERICK' inscribed in gold lettering.

Mr B saw the smile flit across Rufus's face, and at once demanded to know what had been found so amusing.

'I feel as if I have been sent to the principal for a caning, Sir. And I notice we share the same first name.'

Mr B chewed hard on the toothpick and growled, 'This is not a school, boy. This is a blasted jail!' in a way that suggested that he, too, was having trouble getting out. That was an absurd thought. From the way Rufus's escorts had behaved in the presence of Mr B, it was obvious that the latter was a bigwig, perhaps even the governor himself. But Rufus speculated that having to sit behind an empty desk and chew toothpicks all day long must surely be a singular form of punishment.

When Mr B again spoke, he informed Rufus that he had read 'The Story of Drag'. He proceeded to offer words of vigorous discouragement:

'You think your name is Naipaul or what, boy! You think you could write a story and get away scot-free. That will only happen in America, boy. Only in America. But this is not America, you hear me. This is Trinidad.'

By and by, the prison authorities considered the request, and, having sought the advice of the Ministry, concluded that permission should be granted, on condition that the name and present circumstances of the author were not made public. They were confident that such anonymity coupled with the very nature of the story would soon consign it to oblivion.

The decision made Rufus quite distraught. Anonymity was not what he was seeking. But on he went, putting the finishing touches to the letter that was to introduce, and extol, 'The Story of Drag' to the editor of the Sunday paper. 'Your courage in publishing this work of mine,' the letter concluded, 'would be deeply appreciated. But do not publish it out of compassion for me. Publish it because you share my conviction that it will stimulate the mental faculties of your Sunday Magazine readers.'

The editor was more than sceptical about that. But it was not too often that anything written by any prison inmate appeared in any local publication. He knew of so many cases where prisoners in other countries had started or continued a literary career from their cells. He didn't think that 'The Story of Drag' marked the beginning of a serious literary career, but why should his newspaper not be the first in the land to expose to the world the prison writings of a home-grown convicted murderer? With any luck, circulation might even be boosted. If only he didn't have to hide the author's identity!

'Today we are pleased to offer our readers the first instalment of a novel by an exciting young writer, who must, at least for now, remain anonymous.' Below those words of introduction was 'THE STORY OF DRAG' in large type, followed by the text of the story:

CHAPTER ONE

The beginning was the toughest part. Once he got started, the words would carry themselves along on their own self-generating momentum. As what's-his-name had said, the book was already written in his head. He had only to get it all down on paper. The toughest part was the beginning. Yes, sir, the beginning was the toughest part.

Balam felt it coming. Yet another moment of inspiration. Yet another privileged five seconds. The two-headed multicoloured dragon. Not the ordinary run-of-the-mill two-headed multicoloured dragon by any manner of means. Balam's dragon would have stood out in a crowd of dragons. The dragon in the street one was likely to meet would breathe fire or do something equally commonplace. Breathing fire was no fun. Only the most backward of the underdeveloped dragons would be caught dead breathing fire – if such a thing were possible. But dragons had sexual impulses too. Dragons needed sex just like the next non-dragon.

Balam's dragon was a homosexual. Or so Balam thought. All the evidence, said Balam to himself, pointed to Drag's homosexuality. It was not only his walk, not only his voice (because Balam and Drag conversed in many different tongues), not only the actual content of their conversation that told Balam that Drag was a homosexual. One had simply to look into Drag's eyes, as Balam had done. That gleam, that glow in Drag's eyes was the distinctive mark of a homosexual, said Balam to himself.

He began to rub Pinky's elbow. She had warned him never again to wake her violently by shouting her name and shaking her shoulder. To be thus awakened was traumatic even for a grown person. The trauma was no less intense than that suffered by a newborn baby (according to the French genius, anyway) on being slapped on the bottom. Rub the elbow gently and ensure a smooth transition.

Yet the emotional shock of hearing, after as painless an emergence from slumber as could reasonably be expected, that Drag desired Balam, needed Balam, needed Balam desperately, nullified in an instant the pleasant painlessness of the emergence. Resolving herself to patient tolerance, she pleaded with Balam to go back to sleep, pointing out that she had to be up early in the morning and had listened attentively to his reflections on the dragon the previous night. Then, forgetting about patient tolerance, she said:

'It's one thing to let a dragon breathe fire on you, Balam. It's quite another thing to let him sodomize you.'

Pinky didn't understand. To begin with, she had objected to what she felt was a dishonest attempt by Balam to impose a human view of sexuality on the dragon kingdom, arguing that the terms "homosexual" and "heterosexual" had absolutely no relevance to dragons. But, then again, Pinky was incapable of understanding. She was condescending – humouring Balam, trying not to laugh in his face when he talked about Drag. She didn't understand what type of dragon Drag was. She refused to admit that Drag wasn't the standard fire-breathing dragon. All dragons breathed fire, as far as Pinky was concerned, "the same way that all horses neigh and all dogs bark, in accordance with the unchanging laws of the animal kingdom" – Pinky's words, not Balam's.

How unimaginative could one get! No doubt the effect of her convent education, thought Balam to himself.

To Pinky's mind, Balam was merely out to impress. She alone could perceive beneath his expressionless demeanour the smug smile of self-satisfied pomposity, as he replied at parties and other inane gatherings to various inquiries from unconcerned but polite-sounding attendants about the progress of the novel. The progress of what novel? The idiots failed to realize that people like Balam would never in 63 million years complete a novel. Balam couldn't even begin. He had nothing to write about. At least, he had never been able to give her the slightest indication of the content of the proposed novel. She kept telling Balam that he had to have a story-line, a strong plot that would hold the interest of his readers. The simple fact was that dragons did not make ideal novelistic protagonists, she argued. Real-life characters. Nothing but real-life characters. Flesh and blood.

Balam hated to be unkind, and never let Pinky suspect that he had scant respect for her views on literature. BA in English notwithstanding, her powers of literary appreciation were distressingly inadequate. Her most trusted critical insights had been with her since the sixth form. They accompanied her to Liverpool and helped her gain her Lower Second Class. Needless to say, she deserved a First, and had her eyes not begun to plague her in the middle of finals, she would undoubtedly have earned her just deserts. Or so she told Balam, who had listened with apparent sympathy.

But Drag was coming back. He could feel it coming. Drag's seven previous appearances had all given Balam an uncontrollable urge to put pen to paper. "Uncontrollable" was not the word; he had controlled the urge – or, more precisely, the urge had controlled itself, or had been controlled. Yet while he hadn't put pen to paper, he had begun to write. Again, as what's-his-name had said, books were written in the head. Fermentation. Gestation. Unseen, unobserved, constant growth. The day would come when the world would become aware. But not before Drag so ordered.

He was wide awake now. They were all wide awake now. In alphabetical order, Balam, Drag and Pinky. The twenty-first century's answer to the *ménage à trois*. Pinky had resigned herself to the obvious. Balam would make a restless and excessively disruptive bed-mate, unless she gave him a chance to express himself. Maybe she should have become a head-shrinker, and charged him for her services. Professional psychiatric care, with sex therapy thrown in for good measure. Much more interesting than trying to get adolescents worked up over *Twelfth Night*.

Balam had been talking for about five minutes now. She lacked the courage to listen. She lacked the inclination, having heard it all before, having heard the same ideas, presented in a different order and clothed in different words. But for a fleeting half-second, or perhaps longer – definitely longer, all things considered – she had wanted to listen, and had in fact listened. Balam had voiced a new idea. She had long suspected that he was leading up to a new theme, copying himself less frequently, becoming, in a word, original. Now there could be no doubt. A disquieting thought entered her mind. It occurred to her that Balam might not simply be the archetypal literary genius *manqué* that she could smile down on with her disarming benevolence. He might also be insane. He might be psychopathic. She was trying hard to remember where she had read that in every literary genius, *manqué* or otherwise, there was a bit of a psychopath. Perhaps she had heard somebody say it. What did it matter anyway? As usual, somebody had got there before her and thought about it first. Not just a single somebody, but millions of some-bodies incorporated in an apparently singular SOMEBODY.

What was new was that Balam had developed a central theme. The novel would present the case of a young man who captured and domesticated a dragon, and trained it to strangle people. What was also new was the idea of featuring Drag in the novel.

TO BE CONTINUED

Anyone who made a habit of scanning the letters-to-the-editor page eventually came to recognize the names of the frequent letter-writers. Many of the regulars used pseudonyms, some assuming academic titles, such as Professor Maco and Professor Dr Watch Dog, PhD, others going back to the Greeks, such as Herodotus and Diogenes. Between them, the regulars provided commentaries – sometimes outrageous, often pedantic, but never boring – on virtually every event of any significance. It was Rufus's intention to use their letters as a barometer of public response to 'The Story of Drag'. But in this, he was to suffer a grievous disappointment.

Professor Maco continued to rail against the private excesses of public officials; Professor Dr Watch Dog, PhD continued to find fault with the grammar used in the newspaper; Herodotus continued to castigate fellow letter-writers for their ignorance of history; and Diogenes continued to write about this, that and everything. None of these heavyweight letter-writers, and none of the minor scribes for that matter, regular or irregular, so much as alluded to 'The Story of Drag'.

He decided to ask the chaplain for his reaction.

'What did you think of my little story, Father?'

Father didn't understand the question; this was the first he had heard of the little story, a fact that only compounded Rufus's disappointment. He suffered the additional mortification, a few days later, of hearing the chaplain confess to having been confused and puzzled on reading the story.

'What were you really writing about, Rufus?'

Once the initial pain of disappointment had begun to subside, Rufus could afford to take a more philosophical attitude. How many of his companions would ever be able to boast of having had a story published in a newspaper? He, Rufus Linton, would have left some kind of mark. Being in print was a reward in itself. And, who knows? Maybe, one day, some foreign student of Caribbean literature, in search of material for an anthology, would unearth 'The Story of Drag' and have no choice but to include it as the sole specimen in the 'Writings from Prison' section.

So in the end, he was quite undeterred, and was even inspired to try his hand at poetry. His muse was a wasp – the type they called 'Jack Spaniards' – whose life he had spared. Rufus had shown mercy. It would have been all too easy to swat it with a folded newspaper when it had landed on the wall of the cell, before ascending to the ceiling. In the event, a murderous spider gave the hapless Jack Spaniard cause to rue the day it flew into that cell. When the deed was done, the poem already existed and only had to be put on paper:

TODAY	TONIGHT
Came a Jack Spaniard	Returned the Jack Spaniard
Out of nowhere	Out of nowhere
Seeking a spot	Seeking a spot
To build his nest	To build his nest
In my cell	In my cell

TODAY	TONIGHT
Felt I should	A hungry spider
Change my ways	In her web
Clear the cobweb	Caught a Jack Spaniard
From my cell	Who wanted to live
I did not	In my cell

Rufus was well pleased. He read and reread the verses, in the correct order, out of order, right to left, end to beginning – and remained well pleased.

And so was the editor, who, against his better judgement, agreed to read what Rufus melodramatically described in a pleading letter as 'the last will and testament, the final poetical utterance to the land of the living from a cell near the dead'. The poem not only pleased the editor, but also emboldened him. Recklessly flouting the conditions imposed by the prison authorities, he featured the name 'RUFUS LINTON' in bold print, heralding the poem as 'verses of condemnation from a man condemned'.

For the second time, Rufus was escorted into the office of Mr B.

'I have a good mind to give you a clout across your head, boy! You want me to lose my job, or what? Anything else you writing, you better save it for after you dead, 'cause nobody going to see it while you alive. You better mark my words, Mr Writer Boy.'

Rufus brooded over this for several days, and he brooded even more when he noticed a letter to the editor signed 'Diogenes'. It was a rambling complaint about the deplorable condition of public buildings, and in one paragraph Diogenes had written: 'As a certain R. Linton can testify, the prisons are infested with spiders and such other venomous creatures, which may be a good way to punish a hardened criminal. But should we punish our Prime Minister by letting rats multiply and replenish White-hall?'

This was not the sort of oblique recognition he had bargained for. 'A certain R. Linton' indeed! That it should come to this! That the Rufus Linton whose arrest and trial had captured head-lines should be reduced to 'a certain R. Linton'!

Uncle Cyril

It was time to give up the writing business, Rufus thought to himself. Mankind would just have to get by without his *magnum opus*. Besides, would the world have been any different if Tolstoy had never lived? No more reading, no more writing. Just waiting and thinking. And he made another resolution: to make one last effort to find out who his father really was. It was something he couldn't afford to put off much longer. So he asked Auntie Mavis, and she told him. It was Uncle Cyril.

Uncle Cyril. Rufus remembered him. He was one of the people who had been declared *personae non gratae* by the Linton family, but with whom Auntie Mavis still maintained cordial relations. Uncle Cyril and Uncle Clive were the two protagonists in an episode in the family's history that Auntie Mavis often spoke about. While Clive was living in San Fernando, he decided that he wanted to buy a car and drive it as a taxi. He calculated that he could make a lot more money by doing that than by working in the oilfields. It was known that Cyril had money in the bank, for he made no secret of his ambition to go away and study medicine as soon as he had saved enough. So one Easter Sunday, Clive approached him with what looked like a sound business proposition: Cyril would advance $1,300 towards the purchase of the vehicle; in return, Clive would pay him $65 a month out of the proceeds of the taxi business until the principal was refunded, and then $25 a month while Cyril was studying medicine. Clive had worked out all the arithmetic and was ready with all the answers. Cyril agreed to the deal, with Mavis as witness. The car would be on the road by Whitsuntide.

Not seeing the taxi or hearing any word about it, Cyril grew concerned that he would never see his money again. A couple of months after Whitsuntide, he asked Mavis to find out if the vehicle had been bought. It had not. Periodic inquiries yielded the same answer. Clive was 'still working on it'. During the Christmas season, Cyril caught a glimpse of Clive at a party, but the latter made himself scarce. And since Clive lived in the south of the island, and Cyril in the north, their paths seldom crossed. At first, Cyril was too embarrassed, too timid or too stupid to travel down to San Fernando to ask about the taxi or ask for his money back. Or maybe he was hoping that Clive would be filled with shame and come forward with something by way of explanation. When he did finally overcome his embarrassment and summon up the courage to go to San Fernando, he was unable to locate Clive. So the very next time he spotted him – at a cricket match at the Queen's Park Oval – he approached and ventured to raise the question.

Clive was honest. He had hoped to double the money by investing in the horses, and had lost it all.

'So how are you going to pay me back?' Cyril asked.

It may have been partly because West Indies had just lost a crucial wicket and were in a desperate situation. Or it may simply have been that Cyril's question had touched a raw nerve. Whatever the root cause, Clive suddenly and completely lost his temper, and diverted the attention of the fans from the plight of the home team with the outburst:

'Only money, money, money! That is the only blasted thing you could think about? You will be the richest man in the cemetery.'

In the shouting match that developed, Cyril called Clive 'a low-life and a low-class drunk who will never prosper'.

'Mark my words,' he emphasized. 'God will punish you. You will never, never prosper.'

Hardly had Cyril pronounced those words when, to his utter consternation, Clive began to cry. Cyril was so confounded that he returned at once to his section of the bleachers, and left the Oval at the end of the next over. Later that day, he himself burst into tears when he told Mavis what had happened, confiding to her that it had been his lifelong ambition to become a doctor, and that every penny he had saved had been to help him realize that ambition.

In addition to the ignominious defeat suffered by West Indies in the test match, a series of other misfortunes befell Clive in quick succession: a doctor told him that his blood pressure was too high, that rum was killing him and that he must stop drinking; he lost his job with the oil company; his car ran off the road and was a write-off; his son contracted meningitis and nearly died. It wasn't long before he started saying to people about Cyril:

'It's one of two things. He got some priest to burn a candle and pray on my head. Yes, he got a priest to put a light on my head. It's either that or he took my name to some obeah-man. But this is not coincidence. This is some kind of hoodoo or voodoo.'

There was no denying that Clive had sorely disappointed Cyril. Yet there was nothing in the latter's appearance or behaviour to suggest that he was going to be permanently embittered by the experience. His resolve was as firm as ever. He remained determined to overcome the financial setback and further his studies. He just wanted to put the episode behind him and put Clive out of his mind. And when he heard that Clive was accusing him of resorting to obeah, he was profoundly distressed, but tried to maintain his dignity, simply saying that he didn't believe in magic – white magic or black magic.

His distress was mitigated somewhat when Mavis visited him to hand him an envelope from Clive. It contained $2,600 in cash. No explanatory note had been enclosed, and no message had been sent through Mavis. All Clive had said to her was:

'Take this to Cyril. Fast!'

In a couple of months, Clive was putting out word that his jinx had been broken as soon as he had paid Cyril back. As far as the Lintons were concerned, that set the seal on Cyril's reputation as someone best avoided.

Rufus had a vivid memory of the day Cyril departed for England. He had left by ship, and Auntie Mavis had taken Rufus to see him off. Cyril had attempted a few jokes with some Spanish-speaking members of the crew. At one point, he had loudly inquired of a group of them:

'Anybody here speak English?'

To a man, they had shaken their heads and said: 'No, señor', whereupon Cyril had pounced on them with:

'But that is English you speaking there. "No" is English. Only the "señor" is Spanish.'

It had sounded like something he had carefully rehearsed in his mind, and he had laughed gustily at his repartee. The same scene had been repeated at least once in Rufus's presence.

Rufus remembered, too, that a deafening horn had sounded, and a loud voice had come over the public-address system, advising all visitors to leave the ship, and warning that 'all stowaways will be fed to sharks in the Gulf of Paria'. At that, Uncle Cyril had fixed Rufus with his bulging eyes, with a stare that made him blind to everyone else. Then he had patted the back of

Rufus's head affectionately, and admonished him to learn his lessons well, so that one day he could take the same ship to go away and become a doctor or lawyer. On the back of Rufus's head, Uncle Cyril's stubby, rough-textured fingers had felt as if they had been to war. Being patted in that way was something that Rufus had always abhorred, and, as always, he had instinctively drawn away.

Auntie Mavis must have noticed that, for on their way back home, she had asked him:

'Why did you stiffen yourself like that when Uncle Cyril was saying goodbye?'

'I don't like people touching up my head.'

'You are a strange boy,' she had said with a sigh.

As that day so many years ago was brought back to Rufus's mind, it suddenly struck him that there had been something strange about the farewell scene. There had been throngs of merry-makers and well-wishers in the other cabins on Uncle Cyril's deck, and even in the cabin that Cyril was to share with a young man who seemed the embodiment of the introspective scholar. But only Auntie Mavis and Rufus had gone to see Cyril off.

'How come?' Rufus inquired.

'He was always trying to be friendly with people, but he didn't really have many friends,' Auntie Mavis replied.

'And what about the family?'

'He was never in our family,' she said sharply.

In fact, Cyril was on the sidelines of the family, since his brother was married to Linda, Mavis's sister. But especially after all the talk about his being mixed up in obeah, the Lintons had obviously resolved to keep him on the sidelines, and there he had remained.

That didn't prevent him from staying in touch with Mavis. Soon after he reached England, he wrote and gave all the details of his trip across the ocean. His cabin-mate, Benjamin, had won a scholarship to a university in England and had spent most of the time in the cabin studying a chemistry book. Benjamin at first struck him as someone with a remarkably limited knowledge of the world outside books. On the first afternoon at sea, he dragged the young man out of the cabin to have tea in one of the public rooms. As they sat down, Benjamin asked Cyril if they would be able to have Milo tea, a question that made Cyril realize how much work would be needed to educate Benjamin.

'On this boat, they have mostly green tea,' Cyril explained. 'They might have some chocolate tea, but I don't think they'll have Milo tea or Ovaltine tea. And they definitely have no bush tea.'

As it turned out, the waiter had only coffee, so Cyril asked if they could have some green tea. The waiter was gone for over ten minutes, and on his return, what he poured into the two cups was not tea, but boiling water. He had, however, placed a small bag on each saucer. Neither Cyril nor Benjamin had ever been confronted with a tea bag before. Whenever they had had tea, it had come from a teapot through a strainer. But Cyril was confident that he understood the modern invention:

'We have to empty the bag into the water. The tea will dissolve like sugar.'

'How am I going to open it?' Benjamin asked, as he examined his tea bag. The same question had crossed Cyril's mind, yet he felt sure that the bag was designed to be opened quite easily. Benjamin watched him tear it open, empty it into the water, and stir and stir and stir. Then Benjamin had a bright idea. He put his unopened tea bag into his cup and removed it after a few minutes. The infusion didn't smell like the green tea he was used to, but at least his cup was not full of floating tea-leaves.

Cyril guffawed as if he didn't care who was looking at him. When he finally controlled his laughter, he said to Benjamin:

'I am a stupid man, but you are a true scientist!'

At dinner on the second evening, it was Cyril's turn to educate his fellow passengers. A basket of fresh tropical fruit was placed on the table for dessert. Looking around his table, Cyril noticed that the mangoes were being avoided by everyone except an English gentleman, who was tackling a mango with knife and fork. The mango slid across his plate, but, undaunted, he pursued it until he successfully stabbed it with the fork. Eventually, he managed to slice it, but he was obviously uncertain how to proceed. Cyril came to the rescue, leading by example. He put a mango to his mouth, bit into it just below the skin, and peeled it with his teeth and fingers. That was all the encouragement Benjamin needed to come to grips with a large, succulent mango, and soon the Englishman and others at the table followed suit and were joking about the intricacies of dining in a restaurant.

Auntie Mavis used to read to Rufus the most entertaining portions of Cyril's letters, which arrived at least twice a year. Without fail, Cyril would enclose a long letter with his Christmas card. But as Rufus turned his mind back to those letters, he couldn't recall hearing any personal information about Cyril. The excerpts Auntie Mavis read to him consisted mainly of Cyril's observations on the way people lived and talked, accompanied by anecdotes about his encounters, and occasional news about Benjamin's progress with his studies. It now occurred to Rufus that he had no idea how Cyril had progressed with his own studies or what he was still doing in England after so many years.

'He had always wanted to become a doctor, but something went wrong. He's a nurse at a mental hospital in the west of England,' Auntie Mavis told him.

'He could have done that at St Ann's, right here in Trinidad,' Rufus noted.

Having got the address of the hospital from Auntie Mavis, Rufus proceeded to draft a letter:

Dear Uncle Cyril,

I do not know if you have heard about my situation, or even if you will remember who I am. They are about to hang me for killing Carmen Linton. Maybe you remember her. She was my mother. Her sister Mavis now tells me that you are my father. Before I die, I would like to know what you have to say about this.

I remain
Your Putative Son
Rufus Linton

Rufus was not altogether happy with the bluntness of his letter, but he dismissed such misgivings with the thought that beating about the bush was not in order. There was no time for sweet little nothings, and he certainly had no inclination to write an ordinary society letter. It did occur to him, however, that the letter might cause embarrassment to Cyril if it fell into the wrong hands at the hospital in England. He therefore took the precaution of writing 'PERSONAL AND CONFIDENTIAL' in red ink on the envelope. As to the possible reaction of Mr B – or whoever else in the prison administration was monitoring his mail since the episode of the Jack Spaniard poem – Rufus simply could not be bothered.

He took Moby into his confidence, and felt better afterwards, much better than after a talk with the chaplain. He had grown quite attached to Moby, and couldn't bear the thought of the loneliness he would feel if Moby went to the gallows first. That was unlikely; Moby was determined not to hang, and swore that they would have to knock him out, put him in a straitjacket, drug him and drag him to the rope. The grotesque spectacle of hefty Moby thrashing, cursing and spitting all the way to the gallows was more than Rufus was willing to witness. But it might never come to that. Before Moby was brought to that pass, his appeals would have to be exhausted. While he waited, he told his fellow inmates hundreds of times that no one had the right to execute him, because the man he had killed 'needed killing'.

'I will go in your place,' Rufus heard Yank say to Moby. It was an isolated pronouncement from a man who didn't like to repeat himself and who often had Rufus wondering whether his taciturnity was a sign of deep thought or of vacuousness. Yank had no intention of appealing. Rufus, too, was prepared to take his punishment, prepared to take his hanging like a man, like any good, decent, self-respecting murderer. Since he didn't want to cheat the hangman, he was disturbed to learn that various well-intentioned people were trying to get the authorities to abolish the death penalty. There were occasional flurries of articles and letters in the newspapers on the subject. The regular letter-writers were all heard from. Rufus was particularly fascinated by a pedantic contribution signed by 'Herodotus':

> We must earnestly endeavour to find some other designation for the 'derricks' that are so inextricably linked with the development of the petroleum industry in this nation of ours. We must refrain from either honouring or perpetuating the memory of that infamous Tyburn hangman ...
>
> With a view to impressing upon the inhabitants of this nation the utter barbarity of capital punishment, I formally propose that the authorities henceforth install the gallows in Woodford Square. Let the University of Woodford

Square become a place of public execution, the Tyburn of Port-of-Spain. *A priori*, we too have our John Sheppards.

Rufus rather liked the idea of being hanged in Woodford Square, right beside the Red House, where his odyssey of discoveries and troubles had started. So tiny was his universe! The building in which he had been sentenced to death was the very building in which the scanty details of his birth were stored. He would complete a perfect circle by being hanged just outside it. He knew, however, that the realistic question was not 'Where?', but 'When?'.

To some extent, impatience had been banished – but not for good. He wanted it to be over and done with, and there were times when he wanted to speed up the clock and go to the rope the very next day. And then there were times when he couldn't even be bothered to be impatient. Whenever they came for him, he would be ready.

He asked to see the chaplain. It was a troublesome meeting, and they argued a great deal, with Rufus refusing whatever comfort the chaplain attempted to offer. Why was it better for them to hang him than for him to hang himself? And was the hangman not committing a mortal sin every time he did his job? The chaplain didn't pretend to have satisfactory answers, and again retreated into what Rufus saw as evasiveness, never dealing with the question of who could kill without thereby committing a sin. Rufus persisted:

'So you think it's all right in God's eyes because he's only doing his job, like a good civil servant writing a report?'

What type of person, Rufus wondered, would accept such a job? He remembered a boy at school who had struck out with extraordinary violence at another for calling him 'hangman son', the taunter being taken to hospital suffering from concussion, the taunted being suspended from school. He had never returned, and, according to school-yard rumour, his entire family had been relocated in Tobago. In Rufus's mind, there surely had to be a less intriguing explanation, but he had never doubted the veracity of the devastating taunt.

What did the hangman do during the rest of his time? Was he a prison officer regularly assigned to other functions? Or was he an anonymous baker supplementing his income on occasional Tuesdays every so many months? The chaplain, as usual, admitted to knowing nothing.

Rufus hadn't expected a prompt response from Uncle Cyril. He hadn't expected a response at all, but had been hoping against hope. It was therefore somewhat disconcerting for the reply to arrive, as if by return mail, within a couple of weeks. He held the blue air letter up to the light, and could tell that the officials had not bothered to open it. Nor did he.

He discussed it with the chaplain.

'My life is in that letter,' said Rufus, embarrassed at the melo-dramatic ring of his pronouncement.

For once, the chaplain seemed to understand:

'It may be better for you never to open it.'

How many times had he sermonized on the irresponsibility, the thoughtless adventures, the lust, the sinfulness, the unhappy results? There were so many other Rufuses out there, groping for clues, names, identities. True, things had been a lot worse during and after the Second World War. As the calypsonians had documented, the soldiers had come, procreated and gone. Rufus was lucky: at least he had a name and an address.

'Let me have the letter,' he said to Rufus. 'Let me read it first. Let me advise you whether to read it.'

He was pleading. He sounded desperate. But Rufus didn't like the sound.

'This is something I have to do for myself. I'm a big boy now.'

The chaplain, for his part, didn't like the sound of that.

The letter remained unopened for over a week. And then one morning, as soon as he woke up, Rufus opened it, read it and decided what he had to do.

That very evening they found him. It was one of the warders passing by his cell who sensed something wrong.

'Linton!' he called out.

It was to the same General Hospital to which the taxi of his fantasies had rushed his mother that they rushed Rufus that evening. They knew they couldn't save him, but they had to go through the motions. He was as good as dead when they put him on the stretcher at the Royal Gaol.

Of course, an official inquiry was ordered, and duly conducted. It was determined that Rufus Linton had taken his own life by ingesting a copious amount of rat poison. No one was able to determine where the rat poison had come from.

Among Rufus's possessions, the chaplain found the letter from Uncle Cyril, and was finally able to read it:

Dear Rufus,

I was once a young man, as you are now a young man. I did all kinds of crazy things.

About the question you ask, it is possible that it could be so. But nobody ever told me it was so. And I never asked.

Best Wishes,
Uncle Cyril

Printed in the United States
1247000001B/1-72

9 781844 261093